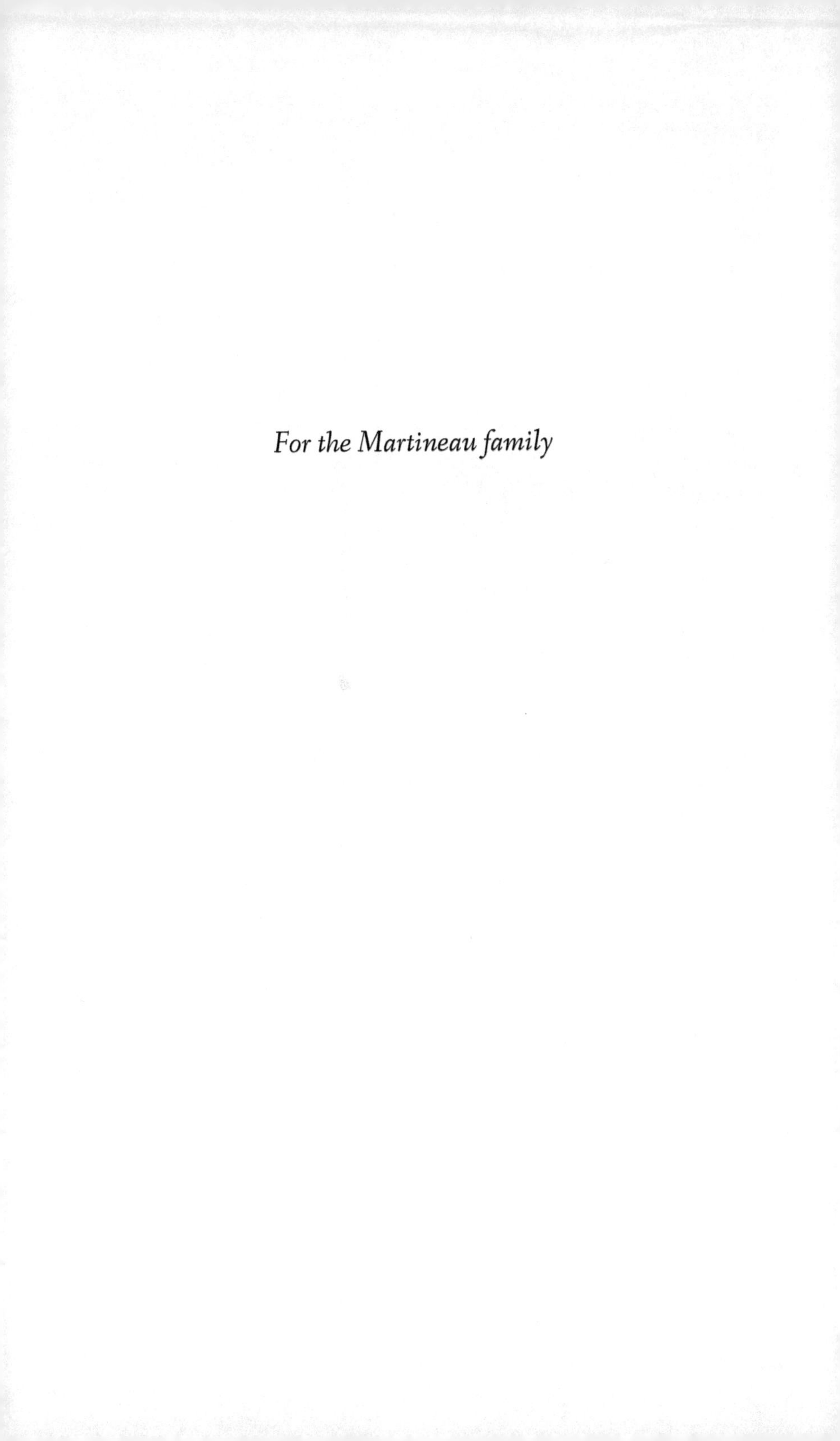

For the Martineau family

It Started with a Sunset

It Started with a Sunset

MEG EASTON

Chapter One

SUMMER

Summer Graham breathed in the sweet morning air as she walked with her roommate from the staff parking lot toward the Student Center. As a student, she'd always lived for summers. As an admissions recruiter at Lake Baldwin State University—her alma mater—summers were the boring part. The part that lacked the energy of students milling all around campus.

This—students walking down the sidewalks, backpacks slung over their shoulders, stopping in groups to chat, hurrying to class, studying under the shade of a tree, setting up hammocks on the quad—was why she worked at a university. "Don't you just love the smell of the first day of fall semester?"

"Nah," Valeria, Summer's roommate, best friend, and ceramics instructor in the Visual Arts department, said.

"You're just still living off the thrill of last night's game night and having so many people hang out at our apartment until so late."

Summer smiled just thinking about it. It was a pretty great night. Being around so many friends, new and old, fueled her like nothing else.

Valeria shrugged. "I prefer the second week of class, personally. That's when we're past the references to the movie *Ghost* in my pottery classes, and we've moved beyond the 'What did Clint Eastwood say before firing the ceramic bowl he made in pottery class? *Go ahead, bake my clay*' joke that someone wants to tell *every single year*."

Summer laughed. "It's definitely been a classic with staying power."

Valeria stopped at the fork in the sidewalks where she and Summer would split up—Valeria heading toward the Fine Arts Center and Summer heading to the Student Center. Valeria fluffed her tight curls, smiled wide, and placed a hand on her curvy hip. "What do you think? Do I look ready to take on a class of freshman art students, while at the same time looking like I'm ready to move up from Instructor to Assistant Professor?"

Summer tapped a finger on her chin like she was actually considering the question when she had no doubt in her friend's abilities or look. "You look like a professional who is small in stature but big in brains and creativity. And hair."

"Like, excessively big hair or exactly right hair? Because I was going for 'make people jealous of my luscious locks,' not 'make them think I stuck my finger in a light socket.'"

"Exactly right hair. You look ready to take on the world."

Valeria seemed to consider it a moment and then nodded like Summer's assessment fit. "Okay, let's look at you. You've got your winning smile, your new, stylin', spunky shorter hair, your LBSU Welcome Center polo, your dark wash professional yet stylish jeans, and —oh, no."

"What?" Summer looked down, panicked. She didn't see anything on her shirt, she hadn't forgotten her lanyard with her school ID, nothing was wrinkly. She looked back at her friend.

"You've got most of the Welcome Center's dress code down, but those are definitely *not* sensible shoes."

It made Summer smile just looking down at her red ankle-strap wedges and then back at Valeria. "But the way I see it, it's my job to help potential LBSU students feel like they could be at home here, right? And people feel most at home when they're around their people. Who is going to represent the fabulous shoe-loving demographic if all of us in the Welcome Center wear sensible shoes? I'm taking one for the team here."

"You're such a rebel."

Summer's smile was broad. "But I'm a rebel in stylish shoes."

And she kept grinning as she walked the rest of the way to the Student Center. She *was* a rebel, and she was proud of it. Well, it was mostly that she just really didn't like people telling her what to do. And that was one reason why she loved working at Lake Baldwin State.

Four years ago, her dad told her that she had one year to finish her degree or he'd stop paying for it. And, okay, she'd been in school for five years at that point, but it wasn't like she'd been wasting those years. There were just a lot of interesting majors.

She'd have finished school at the end of that sixth year even if he hadn't brought it up. But it was the fact that he told her to be done with college that made her find the loophole and get a great job at the university so she'd never have to "be done" with college. And now she got to enjoy being a rebel every day as she took this walk to the Student Center.

In fact, still working at the Welcome Center after three years was a rebellion in a way, too, since everyone expected her to quit and move on to something else challenging by now, since that's what she did with everything. She mastered something and then moved on.

She stopped and took the perfect selfie—with her smiling face in the foreground and the six-foot-high metal letters spelling out Aquamoose in the background, complete with two students posing behind the letters with their faces in the double O's, a friend taking a picture of them.

She captioned it with *Living my best life*, added a few fun embellishments, and posted it. Then she headed into the Student Center and walked down the hall to the Welcome Center, which just happened to be the best part of the entire university. It was where all the excitement was.

She was early, of course—she had to be to get in a morning meeting with the student ambassadors before prospective students started showing up—so there weren't many people in the office yet. But it didn't matter how early she got there, Brock always beat her there. She could see him through the glass wall of his office—already meeting with a student, even.

Coming in early because it was fun was one thing. Coming early because you were a workaholic was unfathomable. She was definitely all-in for the fun.

Although she was in charge of fifty student ambassadors, only five worked at a time on most days. Technically, she and the five of them working today could all fit in her office for their morning meeting, but who wanted to be that squished? So she headed to the big meeting room—it was where they had all the students and their parents meet together before heading off on campus tours, so it was by far the room that was the most Ambassador Territory, anyway.

She should've guessed that Paige and Alejandro would already be there. They were the school versions of workaholics. Schoolaholics?

As she sat down on the table at the front of the room, chatting with the two of them, McKay strolled in, showing the tiniest little sliver of first-day jitters beneath his confident exterior. She heard Takeshi's chortling laugh before she saw him walk in with Jessa, who seemed to always bring a gale force of excited air bursting into the room, swirling around and trailing behind her, and a part of Summer kind of expected a flurry of fall leaves to swirl around in her wake.

Jessa brought that gust right up to where Summer was sitting and said, "Oh, wow, Summer. Those shoes are my new favorite thing ever."

Summer smiled. See? They did help students connect to her.

The excitement in the room was palpable. Summer clapped her hands together. "Are you all ready? Everything you trained for during our retreat last week is starting!"

Yeah, they were excited. They were sitting forward in their seats, eager anticipation on their faces, feeling the bonding they had developed during the four days they all spent in a cabin at the edge of Lake Baldwin, learning leadership skills and everything they needed to know to be an ambassador for the coming year. That was why not only being an admissions recruiter but also being over the ambassadors was the best job ever.

"Okay, since it's the beginning of the year, we've only got one tour that we'll split into two groups. Jessa and Alejandro, you'll each take one. Until they arrive, you two can head to the staging room and work on your plan together. Paige, Takeshi, and McKay, you're at the desk in the Welcome Center lobby, greeting people and hand-writing this week's happy birthday cards to prospective students. Whenever you've got a free minute, quiz each other on all things Lake Baldwin State University. Any questions? Wait...Paige, why do you look like you're about to fall asleep?"

Paige tried to stifle a yawn, then said, "Remember back at that leadership event last summer when we first applied to be ambassadors and you recommended that none of us register for a seven a.m. class?"

"Yes. It's solid advice." Summer gave it to every incoming freshman she could.

"Yeah, I didn't listen."

All four ambassadors shook their heads as if they understood well her folly, even though Jessa was the only one who wasn't a freshman herself. McKay even reached over and patted Paige on the shoulder.

"What?" Paige said. "My high school started at seven-thirty. And I always went even earlier for band, so I thought it wouldn't be a big deal."

It didn't matter what Summer said, there were always kids who ignored the advice. For some, it was just fine. For most, it wasn't. "You've just got to look at it this way: college is in a different time zone. Seven a.m. here isn't the same as seven a.m. in high school."

"I get it now. And I swear I'll listen to every piece of advice you give from now on."

Summer tried to hide her smile.

"No, really," Paige said. "In fact, I'll take any advice you've got right now. Lay it on me."

Summer was full of advice. After all, she had spent six years going to school at LBSU herself. "Okay, schedule homework just like it's a class, and schedule it during the day—not at night when there's fun stuff going on all around you. Don't overload your schedule with too many classes." She heard Alejandro suck in a breath. Clearly, that advice was a little late for him.

"Oh, and Professor Burningham is oblivious to clocks in general and never ends on time, so don't schedule a class on the other side of campus that starts ten minutes after his gets out."

Takeshi slapped both hands down on his armrests. "Now you tell us that? I have him at one, and I've got to be all the way over in Carter Hall at two."

All the others winced, but Summer chuckled. "Don't worry, Takeshi. You've got this."

She stayed and chatted with them, answering all their questions about their ambassador duties for the day, making sure they were all pumped up and feeling confident and ready to go. They were about to be the face of the university for high school kids who were still deciding which college to attend, so enthusiasm was key. At a quarter to nine, she had to end the meeting so they could all get to their places.

As they all left the big meeting room, Jessa hung back, her usual gale of excitement feeling more like a slight breeze.

"You okay?" This was Jessa's third year as an ambassador, so Summer knew it wasn't because of nerves about the job.

"Oh, yeah, totally." Jessa was quiet for a moment as they walked toward the staging room. Then she said, "My roommate said something last night that I guess I'm still thinking about. Do you ever... I don't know. Do you ever feel that it probably appears like you've got everything in your life together to other people, because you do on paper, but there's just something missing and you can't quite figure out what it is?"

Summer let out a breath of a chuckle and nodded. "Yeah. All the time." If she thought about it long enough, she could probably say what exactly that something missing was. The key, though, was to *not* think about it long enough.

"What do you do about it?"

But before Summer could answer, Alejandro came out of the staging room, looking panicked. "Jessa, I'm so glad I'm doing this with you because I'm kind of freaking out and I think I just forgot what every building on campus is named. I suddenly don't even remember where my own classes are."

Jessa turned and smiled at Summer. "Duty calls. We'll talk later."

Summer knew that Jessa was exactly the person who Alejandro most needed just then and that she needed to let her little birdies spread their wings without too much interference from her. So she headed to the lobby and down the other hallway that led to their offices and the other part of her job in the Welcome Center.

But as she walked, Jessa's question hung around, like part of Jessa's gust of wind was trailing Summer now, asking over and over if something was missing in her life and what she usually did about it.

Now that she thought about it, she knew exactly what she did about it. She surrounded herself with people so she didn't have to think about it. Everything was better that way. She grabbed her water bottle from her office and headed to the common area—the space in the middle of their offices, where she could currently see nearly all her coworkers—and cupped her hand against the metal water bottle, hitting her rings against its surface three times.

It was the rallying cry for their team. Or at least the "Let's all go to Aquamoose Crossing, the convenience store down the hall, to fill up our water bottles before the day starts" cry. Her rings hitting against the bottle made the most beautiful, musical sound. A sound that not only drown out any big, unanswerable life questions, but brought everyone together and started the day off just right.

Chapter Two

BROCK

*L*uke, the high school senior that Brock was working with, jumped at the sound of Summer's rings banging against her metal water bottle.

Brock glanced out his glass office walls to the common area, where Summer stood with a grin on her face. "Annoying, isn't it?"

Luke shrugged like he wasn't willing to commit to saying it was. Then his eyebrows drew together. "What's she doing?"

"Calling everyone to go walk as a herd down the hall to Aquamoose Crossing."

"That's actually kind of cool. Do you need to go?"

Brock shook his head and held up his full water bottle as he opened the scholarship page of the school's website that contained every scholarship offered only to LBSU students, along with his spreadsheet where he'd kept track of every scholarship he'd ever found outside of those, all categorized and ranked. "I don't need to, because I came prepared. Okay, I'm glad you're willing to write essays, because that opens so many more scholarships to you, and they're the ones that have fewer students trying for them."

He scanned through the categories, looking for the ones that most fit Luke and his situation, but all the movement outside his office was distracting, especially for Luke. It was one of the drawbacks to having the one wall facing the common area be made of glass. At least he didn't have one of the desks out in the common area that was open to every distraction all the time.

He glanced over the half-wall that divided the Welcome Center from Admissions—a department they worked closely with. Avery Parks, the administrative assistant, was holding her water bottle, quietly poking her head into offices, likely asking if anyone wanted to join her in a trip to the watering hole. No massive distractions like what was going on outside his office, with the chatting so loud, now that almost everyone had gathered, that he could hear it in his office with the door closed. Luke kept turning to watch.

"Look at how nice and calm they do the same thing in Admissions. Maybe I should request a transfer over there."

"No!" Luke's attention whipped back to Brock, a panicked expression on his face. "You can't. I need you here. I have two older siblings—Lily and Logan—do you remember them? They were only able to go to school here because you helped them to get scholarships. I've been working all that I can after school, but there's no way I could ever afford college if I don't get scholarships. I really *really* need your help."

And this was exactly why Brock was where he was at. He couldn't have gone to Lake Baldwin State University without scholarships, either, so he knew well the panic that was showing on Luke's face. There was nothing that brought him more satisfaction than helping someone decide to go to college, decide on getting their degree at LBSU, or helping a student find a way to pay for it.

"And I'm going to help you find what you need." He smiled at the kid. "You've got someone to critique your essays, right?"

He nodded. "My English teacher offered to read through all of them. And my guidance counselor said he'd help, too."

"Excellent." He gave Luke a fist bump. "I'll help find you the scholarships, you work hard on the essays, and you've got this. By this time next year, you'll be an official Aquamoose, heading off to class."

Luke grinned widely at him.

The kid only had one free period at his high school, so they needed to be finished with this meeting in time for him to make it across town for his next class. Not to mention the morning stand-up meeting that Brock had in just a few minutes. The kid's focus was back one hundred percent on Brock. The fact that the herd had left to get their water bottles filled helped.

So they dug in, and just before the kid had to leave to get back for his next class and Brock's meeting started, Luke had in his possession a list of scholarships that he could apply for, ranked by importance, a game plan for writing the essays, and a hopeful smile on his face. He probably thanked Brock half a dozen times as he walked him from his office to the lobby of the Welcome Center.

Brock really did have the best job ever.

He got back to the common area just as everyone was gathering for their morning meeting. Once a week, they met via video call with everyone in the office and the recruiters over other areas in the state and nearby states, but this meeting was just the seven of them. And they did it standing up in the common area—that way, no one got comfortable and the meeting didn't go on longer than absolutely necessary.

He took a spot across the circle from Summer, which was fitting—they seemed to be on opposite sides of most topics. Like a flock of birds, they all turned their attention at nearly the same time toward Elle's office. She had a phone to her ear and held up one finger to them while nodding and slowly bending toward the phone base, like the person on the other end could see that she was in a hurry. Deja left the circle and grabbed a pen off her desk—the only one that sat in the common area—then made it back to the circle just as Elle left her office.

"Okay," Tess, their boss, said as her eyes went from the tablet and stylus in her hands to the group. "I've got to meet my husband to go to an appointment in an hour and a lot to do before then, so I'm going to make this fast. We're going to go around the circle in this direction. Give me a two minute or less update on where you're at and what you've got planned for today. Go."

Everett talked about some texts and emails about visiting campus that were going out to high school seniors that were showing some interest and some partnerships in the works with local businesses to provide some perks, and Elle talked about what stage she was at with some recruitment events.

The whole time, Brock kept stealing glances at Summer. He'd liked her hair when it was long blonde curls, but this shoulder-length style fit her more. It brought out her smile more, somehow. She might drive him crazy sometimes, but that smile of hers was infectious. Everyone seemed to be in a better mood around her. He hated to admit it, but maybe he was, too. Even when she disagreed with him on virtually everything.

She was dressed the same as everyone else—LBSU Welcome Center polo and nice, dark wash jeans, just like the dress code in their employment contracts stated. But unlike everyone else, Summer wasn't wearing the sensible shoes the contract called for. She was flaunting the rules without a care, and right in front of their boss, even. He didn't get it.

When it was Summer's turn, instead of giving an update, she crinkled her brows. "Where's Pavani? Since it's the first day of school, we don't have any events scheduled."

Tess let out a slow breath and then grimaced. "I was going to bring that up at the end. Remember how she was worried that she had either food poisoning or an ovarian cyst last week? Apparently, it was her appendix, and over the weekend, it ruptured. She got to the hospital quickly after that and they did surgery almost immediately."

Summer gasped and her hand flew to her mouth. "Is she okay?"

Tess nodded. "I talked to her this morning. The surgery went well and she seems to be in fine spirits and is recovering, but she's going to be out for two to four weeks."

"We should take her flowers," Summer said.

Deja scribbled in her notebook. "I'll get some ordered and sent to the hospital, and I'll get a card we can all sign."

Tess nodded in agreement.

"No," Summer said, "we should take them to her. All of us."

Brock scoffed. "She's in the hospital, recovering from

something that would've killed her if they didn't do surgery. She needs peace and quiet to recover."

Summer met his eyes. "No, she'll want to know that we care about her."

"She'll know that we care because of the card and flowers." If Brock was in the hospital, the last thing he'd want was everyone showing up and seeing him in recovery. "Pavani doesn't need half a dozen people crowding into her room, making her feel like she is supposed to be working. We should let her rest."

Summer shook her head. "You are heartless. We are each other's work family, and neither Pavani nor her husband have family nearby. Do you know why a hospital has visiting hours? Because people *need* visitors to keep their spirits up so they recover more quickly."

"Do you know why hospitals have quiet hours? Because people *need* peace and quiet to recover from all the people thinking they wanted visitors all day."

"Okay, you two," Tess said, annoyance ever so slightly breaking through her normally professional tone. "I will be talking to Pavani over the phone later today. I'll find out if she wants visitors or not. Now let's focus on the meeting. *Chop, chop!* Summer, Brock, and Deja—you have one minute each."

The meeting finished quickly, but he could still feel some exasperation coming from Summer that was aimed in his direction. Whatever. He was right. Pavani wasn't going to want a crowd.

"Summer, Brock," Tess called out as everyone was heading back to their desks, "I need to see you in my office right now."

And suddenly, he and Summer were on the same side as they walked down the hall toward Tess's office, taking deep breaths, clearing their throats, and sharing worried glances that maybe they pushed things too far this time.

Showing her usual perfect posture and professionalism, Tess sat down behind her desk, so both Brock and Summer moved to sit down in the two chairs in front of it. Before he got a chance to sit, though, Tess said, "Will you shut the door, please?"

Oh. That was not a good sign. He did as he was asked and then took a seat.

Tess placed her tablet on the desk in front of her and then moved it to the side, lining it up exactly parallel to the sides of the desk. Then she took a breath and looked at both of them. "I've got a full morning, so I'm going to cut right to the chase. Having Pavani out of commission at our busiest time of the year is definitely going to be a challenge, and we'll have to get creative with our solutions."

Oh, that was what this was about. Brock relaxed his tense shoulders and rested back into his seat.

"Summer, you and Pavani normally work together on the Aquamoose Tracks overnighter. It's too big of a job to do solo, so Brock, I would like you to partner up with Summer."

Both he and Summer sat forward in their chairs and called out "What?!" nearly simultaneously.

"It makes no sense to have us work together," Summer said. "We have opposing opinions on everything."

Brock nodded. "I'm over financial aid, not events. And I'm the *assistant director*. Why didn't you come to me to discuss options and brainstorm what might work best?"

Tess placed her arms on the desk, fingers coming together and interlocking, looking like the picture of calm professionalism—the opposite of what Brock felt just then. "Because I want you to do it, and I knew you'd say no if you were in on the deciding."

"Remember how great freshman orientation went last week?" Summer gave the slightest breathless laugh like she was hoping that acting like this plan was no big deal would convince Tess to tweak it, but she wasn't really pulling it off. "Elle and I worked so well together on that. It would make the most sense for the two of us to work together on Aquamoose Tracks. This kind of thing is right up her alley."

Tess shook her head. "I have Elle taking over some of Pavani's other responsibilities, even though her plate was pretty full already with the open houses, Sterling Scholars, and details for all the other events we've got coming up."

"What about Everett?" Brock asked.

Tess let out a rushed exhale that was part sigh, part impatient huff. "Listen. We've been talking about mixing things up for the event, right? Aquamoose Tracks always makes the biggest difference in the number of applications we get and is the number one biggest factor in a student deciding to come to Lake Baldwin State. This first overnighter at the end of the month sets the precedence for the five other overnighters we'll run this school year. You two have chronically opposing opinions? Great. I think that's exactly what this event needs—two people who will challenge the way things have been done."

"But—" Brock started, but didn't get any further before Tess cut in.

"Do you think you're not up to the task, Mr. McMillan?"

Of course he was. And she must've seen it written all over his face because she didn't even wait for an answer before she turned to Summer.

"And you, Ms. Graham?"

"I can make the event rock no matter who I'm doing it with."

"Good. Now if you two will vacate my office, I'd appreciate it."

They both let out a huge breath as they left Tess's office. Apparently, he wasn't the only one who had been holding onto some stress in there.

Summer seemed to go straight from exhaling her relief

to inhaling optimism in the span of a single breath because then she smiled that broad smile, clapped her hand against his shoulder, then said, "Well, partner. It looks like we have some work cut out for us. I was supposed to meet with Pavani at three. Does that work for you?"

He couldn't flip from annoyance to optimism so quickly, so he just nodded, and Summer turned and walked down the hall toward her office.

Brock was in touch with himself enough to acknowledge that there was a small part of him that was not fully annoyed about the arrangement. But he had opinions, and he wasn't about to let them get trampled by someone just because she had a great smile.

Chapter Three

At three o'clock, on the dot, Brock knocked on Summer's office door. She waved him in, but he just opened the door and stayed in the doorway.

"Want to meet in my office?"

"Why? We're both already here in mine."

He glanced around her office—a space filled with LBSU swag, pictures of her with friends, padded chairs in front of her desk complete with cute LBSU-colored teal and purple throw pillows instead of the standard boring facilities-provided ones, a couple of office plants, and a giant painting of the view of campus from the Student Center that Valeria had painted specifically for the wall behind Summer's desk. He was trying to act all nonchalant as he looked, then gave a one-shouldered shrug. "Mine just has a little more space."

Summer put a hand on her hip. "Brock, our offices are the exact same size. What are you really trying to say about the differences in our spaces?"

"Mine is just more neat and orderly. Minimalistic. Yours is..."

She lifted an eyebrow, then finished his sentence for him. "Full of liveliness and vitality?"

"Chaotic."

"And yours is a graveyard where ideas go to die. Now take a seat already. I've got everything we might need to plan for Aquamoose Tracks right here."

He glanced at her chairs like he was judging them. Knowing Brock, he wasn't judging their colors or shape or size or overall design—he was judging whether or not she broke a rule or code by using them. For the record, they weren't *exactly* against the rules. When she'd asked to have the boring chairs removed, the guy in facilities had said that they didn't really have any rules on whether or not an employee could bring in their own super stylish and comfy chairs. But it still gave her happy rebel vibes to have them.

"Brock, we can pull a chair from your office if you'd rather not sit in mine."

He must've realized how ridiculous he was being because he took a seat in the one with the fuzzy teal pillow. It was worth it to push for the meeting in her office. She was going to be smiling all the way through it. He would appreciate it, too, when he saw how much more creative this space made him.

Although by an hour into their meeting they had figured out some of the details on the first part, where all the students were together, they still hadn't come to any kind of agreement on the presentations. Summer wanted to show them all the fun stuff they had to look forward to as an LBSU student, and Brock wanted to show them all the boring stuff.

She looked up from her piles of papers and her tablet. "You should go with me on a campus tour."

"Thanks, but I know the campus well already."

Summer rolled her eyes. "Not just me and you. I mean we should take one of the groups of prospective students on a tour. The first week of school is always tough, especially for the ambassadors who are freshmen. They don't quite know what to expect when it comes to classes and the homework load, and there's always at least one ambassador who's supposed to lead a tour group who stresses out and can't make it the first week. When that happens, go with me."

He turned his head slightly, eyeing her, trying to figure out her motivation. "Why?"

"Because I was an ambassador for *six years*, Brock. Long enough to know that those kids ask lots of questions. You'll get to experience firsthand what kind of questions they ask. It's a good way to understand what kinds of things they need in an overnighter."

He smiled like she was playing right into his hands, but she smiled, too, because little did he know that he was playing right into her hands. He had made his way to working in the Welcome Center by starting as an admissions advisor. He didn't know prospective students like she did.

He gave a curt nod.

"Deal."

"Good. Because I'm telling you, Brock, we need to focus on getting them to have fun with each other. To make connections with people who might be their future classmates and with the ambassadors who already know the ropes. If we get them to connect with people here, that's what's going to help them feel like there's a place for them here. And if they feel like this is their place, then they're more likely to choose Lake Baldwin State."

"But that's not the most important thing they need to get out of the overnighter," Brock said. "What does any of that matter if they don't believe that they can get the money they need to go to school here? Then you're just dangling candy in front of them and telling them they can't have it. We need to show them how to get it."

"So you want them to just sit down and do scholarship stuff."

Brock nodded. "I did a campus tour here in September

of my junior year of high school. They said nothing about scholarships, and I knew I'd never be able to go here. I didn't want to keep tempting myself with something I couldn't have, so I stayed away for more than a year until a friend begged me to go with her on a tour so she wouldn't have to go alone. They talked about scholarships that time, and I finally felt like it was a possibility."

"I get it, Brock. I know your job is important. Aquamoose Tracks just isn't the event for it, though. We are supposed to make them feel like they're living a day in the life of a student here, so we need to take them to fun student activities around campus. A big school event, like a football or basketball game or gymnastics competition. Let them check out campus. Hang out with college students, doing college student things. Stuff like that. Not drudgery-type stuff that feels like homework that they can sit at home and do."

Brock leaned back in her comfy chair, his arms folded, his eyes on her. They were pretty eyes—she'd give him that. They were all dark and had the perfect amount of smile crinkles and his dark-framed glasses made him look all studious. But not "studious" like a teenager doing homework on a Saturday night instead of hanging out with friends. More of a "model trying to look studious" studious.

He must've felt her attention being on his glasses for a moment because he used two fingers at his temple to give them a nudge up, and good golly, if it wasn't the most attractive thing ever.

"You mean stuff like actual homework? What is more of a 'day in the life of a college student' than doing something that resembles homework? Social activities aren't the only reason kids go to college. It isn't even the main reason. They go to college because they want to learn. They're coming to this event because they want to learn all about what it'll take to get here."

Okay, he had a point. A small point. But it wasn't like they skipped talking about scholarships altogether—they always took a minute to tell them they had a website page that had all the scholarships listed and gave them info on how to set up a meeting with Brock if needed. They just never did it as a full presentation during the part while the parents were present. And she wasn't convinced that it wouldn't totally bomb.

But she *was* enjoying the verbal sparring with Brock. She and Pavani agreed on most everything, so their planning sessions were more about getting hyped up for it and discussing things that would make it even more awesome. Brock was challenging her and her way of thinking. It was fun. Not that she'd tell Brock that—this had turned into a competition, and she wasn't about to lose any points to him. Plus, she liked seeing the earnest way he tried to convince her of everything.

Just thinking about competing with him sparked something brilliant. "I've got the perfect idea."

Brock's eyebrows rose in challenge, clearly expecting her idea to be anything but perfect.

"We each do a presentation on the part we think is most important. Me on the stuff that's going to make them feel like they belong here, and you about scholarships. We always have them fill out surveys at the end to let us know how we did and what they liked; we'll see which of us gets the higher score." She was thinking things through and making it up as she went, details falling into place as she spoke. "In fact, we'll specifically have them rate each of the presentations on not only how helpful it was, but also how much it helped them make their decision on whether or not to come to Lake Baldwin State."

Brock started nodding slowly about halfway through her proposal, nodding a bit more enthusiastically by the end. "Okay, but neither of us—or anyone else helping out —can encourage students to rate our presentations higher. We don't even mention the evaluations during our sessions."

Summer held out a hand. "Agreed. I'm in."

He leaned forward in his chair, reaching across her desk to shake her hand. "I am, too."

It was a nice handshake. So much so that she might've held on a beat too long, just to enjoy the feel of his hand in hers, and she had to cover up the awkwardness by distracting him.

"But I'm holding you to going on that campus tour with me as soon as someone needs a fill-in."

Brock nodded. "I'll be there with bells on."

She kind of couldn't wait.

Chapter Four

BROCK

Brock was on campus, headed toward the Student Center, when he felt his phone buzz in his pocket. He pulled it out to see a text from his boss.

Tess Barringer to Welcome Center: Pavani is doing well enough for visitors. If you're free at lunch, we can all go over as a group.

He was about to put the phone back in his pocket when it buzzed with another message.

Summer Graham to Welcome Center: [gif of happy dancing]

Deja Wright to Welcome Center: I'll make
sure the flowers are delivered here by then. Y'all
skedaddle on over to my desk before then to sign
the card.

He still didn't think that Pavani actually wanted all of
them in her hospital room, but if they were going to all go,
he'd be there, too. He'd just need to hurry through everything he had scheduled for the morning so he could
squeeze in time to work on the proposal for the website
changes that he had planned to do during lunch.

When he got to the Welcome Center, the door to the
lobby was locked. He smiled as he unlocked it. He loved
when he was the first one in the office. It was so much
easier to get work done when it was so quiet and free from
distractions.

He'd barely gotten his computer booted, his notes out
on the desk and organized, his notebook in front of him,
his hand on his mouse to bring up the school's website and
his word processor when Summer walked up to his doorway, startling him. With as exuberant as she looked, he
couldn't believe she made it in the front door of the
Welcome Center without him hearing a peep.

"Guess what?" Her smile lit up her whole face.

"We get to see Pavani at lunch?"

"Well, yes. *And...*" She dragged the word out like she
was trying to build excitement. "Haley sent me a message

this morning asking if she could get out of her Ambassador duties this morning because she's overwhelmed with school. I thought it wouldn't be until day three or four before we'd get our chance to lead a tour group, but we get it *today*."

He couldn't help but glance down at her teal heels with the chunky straps.

She waved her hand like she was waving away his concerns. "Oh, don't worry, Mr. Rule Follower. I keep a pair of adorable 'sensible shoes' for times like this. So are you excited? Be in the main meeting room at ten-thirty. It's going to be fun!"

Then, as quickly as she had appeared in his doorway, she was gone again. But she'd actually left behind a little bit of that excitement. Enough that he found himself smiling and possibly looking forward to the tour.

But then he looked back at his to-do list. He'd have to work extra fast to get all he had planned done today in his quickly diminishing time.

———

WHEN BROCK STEPPED into the main room at ten twenty-nine, fifteen people, sitting in groups of two or three, were in the first three rows of chairs, facing the screen. Summer and Elle were just finishing the presentation about the school.

He stood next to Leo, a black kid starting his second year as an ambassador. Brock remembered helping him with scholarships before he started at LBSU. He was a smart kid who loved people and hated essay writing, so Brock had recommended that he go to the nine-day Leadership Academy the Welcome Center hosted and to apply for an ambassador position as a way to get a scholarship. It had been a good call.

"Okay," Summer said, pointing at various prospective students sitting in the chairs, "You three will be going on a tour with Leo."

Leo raised his hand and stepped forward.

"They're all considering education-related majors." Summer turned back to the group. "You're all in luck because Leo's working toward his bachelor's in secondary education."

The three students that Summer had mentioned, along with the parents for one, a mom and a younger sister for another, and a friend for the third, got up and walked to Leo before he led them out of the room.

"Okay, and you four," Summer said, spreading her hands wide at the remaining people, which included two prospective students that looked like friends, another with his dad and a fourth with both parents, "get the rare treat of going on the tour with Brock and me."

Everyone looked over at Brock, so he waved.

"I was an ambassador here for six years, and I've

worked in the Welcome Center as a recruiter for three. Brock went to school here, too. He was an academic advisor for three years right after he graduated, then he joined the Welcome Center as a recruiter. He's been the Assistant Director over Financial Aid for a couple of years now. So that pretty much means that we think we have all the answers, and it's your job to ask all your most burning questions until you stump us."

Brock chuckled as he saw the looks of determination on their faces.

"Alright, then, let's head out."

He mostly let Summer do all the talking. She had probably been an ambassador longer than anyone in Lake Baldwin State University history, and she was a pro. As soon as they stepped out of the Welcome Center into the hall, she talked about all the different places in the Student Center and all the resources available to them. She was great with the students. They seemed to immediately connect with her, and asked questions non-stop, really taking her challenge to heart, apparently.

When they walked past the big metal letters in the lawn just outside of the Student Center that spelled Aquamoose, she told them about how they got their mascot, Baldy the Aquamoose. "A couple was out walking along the path that circles the lake and they said a creature rose out of the water that looked just like a moose, antlers and all, but was much larger and had scales instead of fur.

We like to debate here whether he got the nickname 'Baldy' because of the scales or because he was spotted in Lake Baldwin."

The mom in the group raised her hand, and sounding slightly worried, asked, "Do you have many moose around here?"

"Only if you count the stands inside the stadium during a Lake Baldwin State football game." Summer winked. "As far as real moose, though, we don't get many at all, which makes spotting one even more of a legend."

Once they headed toward the library, she said, "Abby, have you decided on a major?"

The blonde high school student shrugged. "Kind of? Actually, I'm having a hard time deciding between Graphic Design and Business Management."

Summer nodded, walking backward so she was facing the group like it was as natural to her as walking forward. "Are you good at art, drawing, creative stuff?"

"I guess. I mean I really like doing it. I don't know if I'm good at it."

The Latina girl walking with her said, "She's amazing. You're going to have to trust me on that because Abby never does."

"Good. That'll make it much easier. I had graphic design as my major for a semester. I can barely draw stick figures, so I guess I should've known it wouldn't work out."

All the people in the group chuckled, and so did Brock.

"Business Management is a good one, too. Professor Ryerson is incredible, so if you go for that major, make sure you take some classes from him. I think I learned more from him in the semester that I majored in business management than I did in any other semester."

Brock's eyebrows drew together. *Huh.* So she had two different majors that she only kept for a single semester?

"Emilio, have you chosen a major?"

"Yep. At least I think so—Finance."

"Oh! That was Brock's major. Brock, do you have any advice for Emilio?"

"Yeah. There's only one professor who teaches Financial Institutions and Markets, and he's tough." Brock shook his head just thinking back to it. "And he assigns a homework load that will nearly kill you. For the semester you take his class, only take half the number of credits you normally take. Trust me on this."

Summer's eyes went wide. "It's really that intense?"

Brock nodded.

Emilio pulled out his phone and started taking notes.

She turned to Brock. "I'm glad I hadn't been interested in finance enough to declare it as my major. Bullet dodged." Then, turning back to the group, said, "What about you, Luciana?"

Abby's friend stood a little taller when she said, "Computer Science. I've been taking programming classes at my high school, and I'm really good at it."

"Nice!" Summer said. "That's one of only two subjects I majored in that I did for a full year. If you're like me and like guys, you're in luck, because the classes are something like eighty percent male. I'll show you the building where you'll be having most of your classes a little later in the tour. Jake? What about you?"

"Communication. Did you have it as a major?"

"Good guess! I did, but only for one semester."

"Oh." Jake's face fell. "It was that bad?"

"No. I switched majors because one of my roommates was taking anthropology and it sounded fascinating. But Communication was great. LBSU has four different emphases for that major, so you can really find what you're going to most love. Okay, now this is the Burningham-Steele Library. Let's go inside. There are a few things I want to show you."

"Wait," Abby said, stopping in her tracks. "How many majors did you have?"

Brock had been wondering the same thing. How did he not know what degree she graduated with? He thought he knew it for everyone in the Welcome Center.

Summer looked up for a moment like she was counting. "Nine." She ticked off each one on her fingers as she named them. "I also majored in Economics, Geology, Philosophy—which, honestly, I was ready to switch out of by midterms—and Sociology. I did that one for a full year."

The looks on everyone's faces—including the three parents present—were of confusion and shock. Brock was glad he was at the front of the group because then he could see that he wasn't alone in that emotion.

"But *why?*" Luciana asked.

"There are just so many interesting things to learn here! I wanted to learn them all. You'll see when you start going to school here next fall—you'll get the learning bug and will want to know everything. I was fortunate enough to have been able to indulge that curiosity. I would've been a forever student if given the choice, because then I could've had all the majors. My dad told me I had to be done with school by the end of my sixth year, though, but the joke was on him because I started here full time the moment I graduated."

Then she led them into the library, and Brock joined in the rear. Mostly because it took him a moment to recover from his shock and surprise. He wasn't entirely sure what he even thought about it. All he knew was that he felt ever so slightly pulled toward Summer.

Not that he wanted to be pulled toward Summer. He was a perfectionist and Summer most definitely was not. If they were to ever date, they'd drive each other as nuts as... Well, as nuts as they drove each other just being coworkers.

They visited each of the common buildings and some of the buildings where the students would likely have classes and then headed back to the Student Center, where they would end the tour and the prospective students would go have lunch in the cafeteria. The entire time, the students and parents were firing off one question after another, trying to get to the point where they could stump Brock and Summer.

But between the two of them, they had answers for all of them so far. They had just fielded quite a few about housing, including which dorms they had lived in, when Jake asked probably the fourth question relating to events on campus.

And, like the other three times, Summer gave Brock a "See? I told you" smile. Okay, so maybe the students did care about campus events and which housing had the most social opportunities. He was silently begging one of them to ask about scholarships.

Then Emilio did, a little sheepishly. "What if we...you know...don't quite know how to pay for college yet. Is it hard to get scholarships? My grades are fine, but they aren't going to give me a full ride or anything like that."

Honestly, with a planned major in finance, he was surprised it took Emilio so long to ask.

His mom added, "He's been pretty worried about that."

He caught a small wince from Summer before he

clapped Emilio on the shoulder. "My man, Emilio. I'm glad you asked. When we get back to the Student Center, I've got some things to share with you. All of you." Then he looked at Summer and gave her his own "See? I told you" smile.

And he kept smiling as he answered the next five questions, which were all about scholarships.

Right as they got back to the Student Center, Luciana said, "Okay, I've got one last question. Are there any famous people who went to Lake Baldwin State?"

"Lots," Summer said. "In every field. The one you'll probably know the most is Declan Davenport."

"The YouTuber?" Abby asked.

Both Brock and Summer nodded, and all the group seemed star-struck. It was a good question to end on; students were always so impressed that Declan Davenport had been an Aquamoose.

As all the prospective students and parents dispersed, Brock kind of marveled at how connected he'd felt to the group after having only spent an hour with them. He'd gone on tours as a prospective student himself, and he'd filled in as a tour guide at least a dozen times over the four years he'd worked in the Welcome Center, but it had never felt like that. Bringing people together seemed to be a skill that Summer had in spades.

She walked over to him, and they headed through the door leading into the common area outside of their offices together. She seemed even more energized by the tour, even though he was feeling a bit drained from it. "I swear the scholarship question doesn't come up every time."

He smiled, kind of amused, and said, "Sure," dragging out the word like he didn't quite believe her. "And how often does your switching to nine different majors come up?"

She lifted a shoulder. "Pretty much every time. It always horrifies the parents, but I think it opens the kids' minds to possibilities they haven't thought of. Maybe."

"And what did you end up majoring in?"

"General Studies."

"You have a Bachelors of *General Studies*?" Did she not care about how that would look on a resume?

"Well, I had enough credits that I could've finished two different majors in that time, but geology had been calling my name, so I decided to do a semester of that first and take General Studies as my major. Besides, I think that major fits me."

He didn't understand that at all. How did she even manage to get letters of recommendation from faculty members? Didn't she worry about making connections that would help in her future career? Her path through school was like throwing all the rules and expectations out the window.

Which really made him worry about this huge event that they were supposed to plan together. "We need to get together soon to make plans for Aquamoose Tracks. I've been making notes, but it's going to take a lot of work to pull it off perfectly."

"Perfection is a myth."

It felt like she'd ridden up to him on a horse, like a knight of old, and stabbed him in the chest with a lance. Perfection was what he strove for daily.

"Things are always changing," Summer said. "The target is always moving. What students need today is different from what they needed last year or when we were students, and it'll be different a year from now."

"That doesn't mean you shouldn't shoot for hitting a bullseye. Anything less than striving for perfection is just being lazy."

"No, you do your best to improve over the previous time and make the next time better. *That's* the goal. You've got to take the ready, fire, aim approach."

"What? Summer, you aim first. 'Ready, *aim*, fire' is a thing for a reason."

"Nope. Not effective, because there are other factors that you can't always anticipate that affect where on the target you'll hit. So you fire, see where it hits, then adjust. Ready, fire, *aim*."

He just shook his head while walking back to his office. Planning this event together was never going to work out.

Summer called out to his retreating back, "Don't forget to sign the card for Pavani!"

Without even turning back around, he said, "Do you really think I haven't already?"

As he was shutting his office door, he heard her say, "True. You probably had the exact time to do it already scheduled in your to-do list."

He smiled as he sat down. Of course, he had. He drew a neat line, crossing Campus Tour off the to-do list he'd rewritten after Summer had thrown a monkey wrench at his previous to-do list. It looked so nice with each item above it crossed off just as neatly.

Chapter Five

SUMMER

Summer was the first one through the door into Pavani's hospital room, and she went to her bedside and gave her friend the tightest hug she dared give her. Pavani's normally tawny skin had more of a gray undertone, and her dark hair looked like she'd spent a rough few days in a hospital bed.

But she was smiling at all of them, and her sweet husband, Zain, was sitting in a chair by her side.

Everett brought in the vase of colorful flowers and set them on a stand beside Pavani's bed with a couple of other flower arrangements.

"It's so good to see you all! Oh, I've missed you all so much. I can't believe I missed the first day of school, too!" Pavani might not be feeling well, but she did seem to perk up at seeing everyone. Summer smiled just knowing she'd been right and Brock was wrong.

Tess stepped up to Pavani's bed and squeezed her hand. "Don't you worry about anything other than getting rest."

"Yes, get rest," Deja said, "and then you milk this surgery for all it's worth, girl. You want to sit in bed all day and read or binge-watch Netflix? Call it 'necessary for recovery.' Want your cute hubby to go get you ice cream? Call it 'necessary for recovery.'"

Pavani nodded. "Got it. Okay, I'm going to need daily updates on how things are going at the office. It's necessary for recovery."

Summer laughed hard. She would probably be the same way. "I'll text you every day."

"I will, too," Elle said. "I'll give you the details I know Summer won't think of."

"Brock?"

Brock looked a little uneasy about checking in with the person whose job he was taking over, but he appeared to understand. If he had a project that was important to him, he would probably want reassurances that they were doing it as perfectly as he would. He gave Summer a quick glance, then looked back to Pavani. "I'll keep you updated on all the decisions we make for Aquamoose Tracks."

Pavani visibly relaxed, an exhausted smile on her face. "You are all the best. But still, I'm just missing so much!"

She motioned at Summer. "I even missed out hearing about your weekend dates on Monday morning."

"I went out with this guy I met at the tri-town meet-up at the lake— Dylan. He's from Golden Springs and it was no big deal."

Why was she suddenly feeling so awkward talking with her coworkers about her weekend date? She'd done it every week before now, and it had never been awkward. Then she caught Brock's eyes and realized it was because she wasn't okay with talking about it around him anymore. She wasn't sure what to make of that realization.

They all talked and joked for a few minutes, and Pavani told them all about her surgery and the drama leading up to it. Every once in a while during their chatting, Summer snuck a few glances at Brock. A few times she had caught him looking at her, and she immediately averted her gaze. Why was catching him looking in her direction causing such a fluttering in her stomach?

Tess glanced at her watch. "We've got to get back to the office soon. Do you need anything before we go?"

"I do. I need a Summergraham."

Summer's face immediately heated and she could feel everyone's confusion at the odd phrasing of the sentence and her name being used as a single word.

Eyebrows knit together, Elle asked, "What's a Summergraham?"

Summer let out a slow breath. "Okay, I'll explain it

the same way I did as an only child who never had enough people around and constantly sought ways to connect to everyone I came in contact with: It's like a singing telegram but full of sunshine. And performed by Summer Graham, of course." And then, just like she did as a kid, she did jazz hands in an arc over her head, like a rising sun. "But no, I'm definitely not doing it in front of you all."

Everyone made various *aww* sounds of disappointment. Except for Brock. He was giving her an amused smile—something she hadn't seen coming from him before.

"Then stay after everyone leaves and do it," Pavani suggested. "*It's necessary for recovery.*"

Summer shook her head. "I can't. I drove Elle and Brock."

"The five of us can squish in my car for the drive back," Deja said. "It's fine—you stay and do your sunshine thing."

Summer waited until everyone had a chance to get at least halfway down the hall before she turned to Pavani. "I can't believe you asked for a Summergraham."

Pavani shrugged, a way-too-innocent smile on her face. "What? Deja told me to milk recovery for all it's worth. I'm just doing as I'm told."

"Okay, I'll give you that. A ruptured appendix definitely calls for a Summergraham. I would normally pick a song and change the lyrics to fit the situation, but with no warning, I'm going to have to go with the standard Summergraham from my childhood. And by childhood, I mean I literally wrote and choreographed this when I was seven years old, so don't expect anything better than what a seven-year-old can do."

"I've been waiting my whole life for this moment," Pavani said. "Well, not my whole life, but I've been waiting for a moment worthy of a Summergraham since you first told me about them last year."

Summer shook her head. She was going to have to stop telling people the story. "You're minus a body part now, so I guess you earned it. Okay, well, I hope it's all you hoped it would be." She took a deep breath and then started singing, doing all the dancing motions as she went. "If you're feeling less than fine, your stress is up to nine, something's hard and you want to whine..." She turned around in a circle and jumped in the air, arms and legs out. "Maybe what you need is some sunshine!

"If you're feeling kind of gray, if you're not doing okay, if you're sick and can't go play, I am here to brighten your day!" She couldn't believe she was still remembering all the actions. The cheesy lyrics, though—those would probably always be burned into her mind.

She took a deep breath before heading into the final verse. "I want you feeling as happy as a guppy, as strong as a gorilla, as loved as a puppy, as cute as a chinchilla. So put up your 'I'm happy' sign, because now you're as warm and bright as summer sunshine!" She finished with her hands out, her best flourish of a finish.

Zain was cheering and Pavani was wiping laughing tears from her eyes, saying, "The laughing! It hurts my incisions!" But she kept laughing, holding a pillow on her stomach.

Then Summer heard clapping from behind her and whipped around to see Brock in the doorway, awkwardly holding the card they'd all signed as he clapped.

"You saw that?" Summer's eyes were wide.

He shook his head. "I swear I just got here." But the smile on his face told her that he caught at least a bit of it. "When we got back to Deja's car, we saw the card on her dashboard, and since I have the longest legs ..." Then, after seeing whatever expression Summer was currently showing on her face, he said, "Okay, I'm going to go now. Get feeling better, Pavani." And then he turned and left.

Summer put her hands on her warm face and sat on the bottom edge of Pavani's bed.

Pavani wiped the last of her laughing tears and said, "That Summergraham was by far the dorkiest, sweetest, funniest thing I've witnessed. I think watching that might have made the whole rupturing of my appendix worth it."

Summer smiled. "Then I guess it was worth embarrassing myself."

Pavani cleared her throat and took a few deep breaths. "Now tell me what's happening between you and Brock."

"Nothing is happening."

Pavani shook her head. "You've both been giving each other looks the whole time you've been here. And that look he gave at the end of your Summergraham? *Mmm.* Yeah, he definitely gave looks then."

"I can confirm," Zain said. "Brock was, indeed, giving you looks."

"I don't know what's going on with us. Honestly."

"I'm just doing the math here," Pavani said, "and trust me, that's not easy when recovering from surgery, but your final year as an ambassador was his first year as a recruiter, right? So you've worked together a while, and you've never looked at each other like that before. What changed?"

Summer lifted her shoulders in a shrug. "I don't know. We were just assigned to work together on Aquamoose Tracks yesterday. We met at three, just like you and I were going to, and I made him meet in my office. Partly because his office is so boring and partly because I just wanted to see him squirm a bit in mine. There was just something about him being in my space and looking as adorable as he always is."

Zain nodded. "He is one very nice-looking man."

"Right? And then we were arguing over what we should do, and I don't know. There might have been a tiny little spark. And maybe a little zing. A flurry in my stomach. But I'm *not* going to date him, because you know my track record with dating. A month from now, we'd be broken up, and work would be awkward and no one wants that."

"Well, when I say I want updates, I definitely mean that I want updates on the status of you and Brock."

"There aren't going to be any updates to give you."

"And I mean daily. And also updates about working together on our baby, because I really need updates on that, too."

"Or more than daily," Zain said. "She's only been away from work for a day and a half, but she's already showing signs of major withdrawal."

"True. And Summer?"

"Yeah?"

"I'm glad Brock is working on it with you. Because it's too much for one person, and I'm definitely not going to be feeling well enough to help you anytime soon. And Brock is on top of everything, so I'm sure he'll be great." She paused a moment, then said, "For the event, and for you."

Summer met Pavani's eyes and held the gaze, so she'd know she's serious. "Don't worry about Aquamoose Tracks at all. We've got this. But Pavani, nothing is happening between me and Brock, so work on coming to terms with that so you aren't disappointed when there are no updates about 'us' for me to give you."

Pavani nodded.

"You're not planning to work on coming to terms with that at all, are you?"

"Nope!" Pavani said cheerfully. "And I don't think you should, either."

Chapter Six

BROCK

From the passenger's seat of Summer's car, Brock glanced over his shoulder to see if there were any police officers nearby when Summer went through a second yellow light that she really should have stopped at. Then his attention went to the parking stalls as they turned onto Main Street. They had a lot of shopping to do for the supplies they needed for the activities at Aquamoose Tracks. Hopefully they'd be able to find everything in the shops here instead of having to drive all the way to Sioux Falls.

Most of the parking spots were full. After a quick glance down both sides of the street, he wasn't sure they'd be able to find one at all.

"There's one!" Summer said as she whipped into a spot between two larger vehicles—a spot he hadn't even seen. He held onto the handle just above the door to keep from being thrown into her with the speed she took the corner at.

"This one is thirty-minute parking, though."

She waved off his concern and said, "It's totally fine," as she got out of the car. So he got out, too, and they headed past a few shops to Taheny's Toys, because they usually had a lot of outdoor summer items. He hoped it wasn't too close to autumn to still have what they needed.

It felt so different walking down the sidewalk in the middle of town right beside Summer. For as long as they'd worked together, they'd never done much outside of campus. She'd always been such a staple of his work life that it was strange to have her here, in a space that was distinctly his personal life. Like his two worlds were colliding.

But it was also kind of nice. And, as abnormal as the moment felt, it also felt, strangely, *normal.*

As he held open the door, Summer stopped as she was walking into the store, turning to him and asking, "Did you bring the list?"

"Of course." He had printed a copy that was in his back pocket, he'd emailed himself the list, and he had it in his notes app. Being prepared was how he lived his life.

He hadn't been in this store for quite a while, but from what he remembered, most of the outdoor summer toys were along the left side and along the back. But it looked like they had brought everything they still had to the front of the store and it was all on clearance. That was going to be great for their budget.

But instead of heading toward the outdoor toys, Summer ran to a bin of dress-up hats and put on a pirate one, then grabbed an old-time sheriff's one and put it on his head. Fitting that she would choose the rebellious one and give him the rule-follower one.

"We need to send an update to Pavani. Come in for a selfie."

Brock moved in close to Summer so they would both be in the frame of the camera—close enough that he could smell her shampoo or perfume or maybe it was just Summer's natural scent—and she smelled just like a bright, sunshiny day, which was pretty much exactly what he expected her to smell like.

So maybe it wasn't her actual scent and more of who she was. Maybe it was like when he was a kid and his mom bought the mystery Kool-Aid that was a different flavor than what its color was, and when his eyes saw that it was grape colored, his tastebuds thought it tasted like grape and couldn't be convinced otherwise. Because it was Summer he was smelling, his brain automatically interpreted the scent as sunshine.

Whatever it was, it was a bit intoxicating.

"Aww, look how adorable we are!"

As he saw their two smiling faces with their dress-up

hats so close together in the picture, he couldn't agree more. "Do you think she feels like she's been getting enough updates from all of us for the past week?"

Summer shrugged and put her phone in her pocket. "I think so, but she's still going stir-crazy. She said she's not used to sitting around doing nothing and it's giving her cabin fever." Then she gasped. "Do you know what we should do for one of the activities? Mystery bag skits! We could get a bunch of random things, like these hats, maybe find some things around the office ..."

Brock took the hat off and put it back in the bin. "Summer. We have room for three activities, and we already decided on all three." It wasn't like they'd decided on a whim and it was still open for discussion. They had spent hours narrowing it down to three that would have the greatest chance of accomplishing their goals—getting the prospective students to get to know the campus, getting them working together, and doing activities that would appeal to the widest range of people.

She took a resigned breath, nodded, took off the hat, grabbed a shopping cart, and then headed toward the outdoor toys, but not before saying, "Spoil sport."

He chuckled, and as she pushed the cart, he took the list out of his pocket. "Okay, it looks like they might have close to the number of pool noodles we need. But maybe we should get all the other items before getting those."

Summer tossed an eighteen-inch inflated plastic ball

at him, and he barely looked up in time to catch it. "They've got plenty of balls. Do we want those, or should we just get balloons?"

Now that Brock was looking at the metal frame filled with balls and seeing how much space they actually took up, he was definitely rethinking the ball idea. "Maybe balloons, so we don't completely fill the staging area and drive everyone nuts for the next couple of weeks."

Summer bit her bottom lip as she looked at the balls, both hands on her hips, surely thinking about the obstacle course they were planning for. All he could do, though, was think about her bottom lip. He had worked with Summer for a long time—why was he suddenly noticing things like her lips? Or how great she always looked in her Welcome Center polo and jeans? Or how she looked just as great in her heels as she did in the actual sensible shoes she wore today?

"I just worry that we won't be able to keep the balloons in place, especially since they'll be going through the obstacle course blindfolded. An obstacle that can be kicked away with barely a touch isn't much of an obstacle. Why would the teammates of the person going through the course even worry about directing them around it?"

"True..." Brock said. "What about using gallon jugs of water instead?"

"Oh, perfect! Great idea."

"Did I really hear you say that I had a great idea?"

She just winked and said, "I call it as I see it." And somehow, that little sentence—or maybe it was the wink—caused his heart to speed up.

As they made their way around the store, she stopped and talked to every person. And not just in a "Hi, how are you doing" kind of way—she seemed to know all of them and asked personal questions about their lives.

"Do you know *everyone* in this town?"

She made a sound that was somehow both a laugh and a scoff. "No, not everyone." She paused for a moment, then added, "I only know the adults."

He was probably visibly gaping at her when a man who was about fifty got out of his car right in front of the shop and walked through the front doors. Summer pointed at him. "I don't know that guy."

Brock glanced back out at the man's car and noticed the out-of-state license plates. "Probably because he's from Nebraska."

"Oh. That's why. Should we go say hi and introduce ourselves?"

He was pretty sure she was just kidding.

Well, mostly sure.

They got some light rope to tie the pool noodles together to make arches and obstacles and then headed over to a shelf with boxes of garden stakes that they planned to use to help stand up the pool noodles as needed.

As they were counting out the sticks, Summer glanced up at him for a moment, then tried to say in a casual way, but didn't quite succeed, "So, have you decided what you're doing for your presentation?"

A smile tugged at his lips. "I have. But I'm not going to share my secrets." All the prospective students and their parents would get the information on the scholarships that the school offered based on their grade point average and their ACT or SAT scores in the packets they gave out at the beginning.

What he really wanted to talk about, though, was the page on the Lake Baldwin State website that he'd helped develop that made it easy to apply for all of the private scholarships in one place. He was hoping he'd find a kid in his presentation who had already applied, been accepted, and knew his login information. Then he'd have them apply for scholarships right in the session, showing it on the big screen, so they could all see how easy it was.

"Oh, I see. Okay, mister, keep your secrets." She held out her hand. "Competition on."

He shook her hand. "May the best presentation win."

She gave him a smile that told him he might have unleashed a pretty tough competitor with that comment. A part of him really couldn't wait to see how it turned out.

They headed over to the hula hoops that they were going to tie from the trees in the area of the quad where they'd be doing the obstacle course, and Summer tossed one to him. And then she somehow convinced him to have a hula-hooping contest right there in the store. And he somehow didn't hate it. In fact, he was actually kind of having more fun shopping than he possibly ever had.

As they got everything in the cart and headed to the checkout stand, Summer saw some 16-foot jump ropes on a shelf and picked one up. "We should get these! We can tie them between two of the gallon jugs, and they can be an obstacle they have to step over. Or tie them between garden stakes at different heights so it's more of a challenge. They have eight of them, which is perfect."

"We didn't plan for them in the budget."

"Everything's on clearance, so we don't have to worry about that."

"No, that'll just give us a buffer for the other expenses."

"We have plenty of money for it."

"I'll tell you what—if we get everything for the event paid for and are still under budget, we'll get the jump ropes."

She narrowed her eyes at him but didn't say a word. She just put the jump rope back on the shelf and pushed the cart to the check stand. The clerk started ringing everything up, and Summer said, "And we'd like all the pool noodles you've got. Oh, and can we borrow the cart for a few minutes to get them all out to our car?" She glanced back at the bin of pool noodles. "Or maybe two carts."

A few minutes later, they were back out on the sidewalk, each pushing a cart filled with hula hoops and garden stakes and rope and pool noodles of every color squished in tight, rising more than six feet high, and they were both trying to peek around the sides of the carts since they were completely blocking their view.

Summer stopped her cart with a gasp, and Brock looked over, alarmed. But nothing seemed wrong—she was just staring at a dress in a shop window that they had somehow not noticed on their way to Taheny's. "Isn't that the most beautiful ball gown ever?"

"Yeah. It's nice." It was a rather happy shade of yellow, and poofed out really big in the skirt part, like a princess dress in a movie. It had shiny beads sewn in it, too. It was every bit as sunshiny as Summer was, and he was already imagining her in it.

"I so want it."

"But it's impractical. Where would you ever wear something like that? Come on, our thirty minutes for the parking space are about up. Let's get this stuff loaded into your car."

Summer threw him a look before turning back to the dress. "That thirty-minute time limit is much more flexible than you are. We aren't going to get a ticket."

"No, of course we aren't." Nowhere in Lake Baldwin

City were there meter checkers—it was only a problem if a shop owner reported that a car had been there forever. "It's more of an unspoken contract, and by parking there, you're agreeing not to break that contract."

"I want to try it on."

The timer on his phone went off just then. Their thirty minutes were definitely up. "No, we've got to go." He knew as soon as the words were out of his mouth that they were the wrong ones. It wasn't the first time in the past week that the two of them had clashed over him being a rule-follower and her being a rule-breaker. As soon as he said it, she turned her shopping cart and pushed it through the doorway into Best Dressed, the tall pool noodles brushing the top of the doorway as she did.

So, he sighed and pushed his cart full of pool noodles and other supplies into the dress shop, too.

Summer was telling the shop owner that she wanted to try the dress on, and the shop owner was telling her how it was the perfect shade of yellow for her and how much it was going to bring out the undertones in her blonde hair. And then Summer was back in the dressing rooms trying it on, and he was standing near them with two overfilled Taheny's carts that seemed so out of place among all the formalwear.

Then Summer came out of the dressing room wearing the dress and he stopped breathing. He was so used to seeing her in a Welcome Center polo and jeans that seeing her wear something so fancy was so foreign to him. She looked incredible. Beyond incredible—he didn't even have a word for it.

The shop owner led her to the small stand in front of the wall of mirrors that had some angled at the sides so she could see more of the dress. From where he stood, he could see how it looked on her from all angles. He'd figured out how to breathe again, but he was still gaping. And, if he was being honest, imagining actually being at a ball, dressed in a tux, dancing with Summer. He knew that mental image wasn't going to be leaving him anytime soon.

The shop owner was cooing and telling Summer how beautiful she was and he couldn't agree more, even though it wasn't out loud—he might have figured out how to breathe, but he hadn't figured out how to speak again yet.

Summer lifted the dress as she stepped off the small stand, and he breathed a chuckle as he saw her gray and teal canvas sneakers. The one time she was actually wearing sensible shoes, and it was also the time when she was wearing a formal gown.

"So," the shop owner asked, "do you have a special event coming up?"

Summer glanced at Brock, a sly smile on her lips. "No, more like everyday occasions."

The shop owner looked understandably confused.

"But I love it, and I want to buy it."

Now he and the shop owner were both shocked. She recovered first. "Well, okay, if you would like to head in and change, I'll start ringing this up."

But, surprising them both further, Summer shook her head. "I'd like to wear it out of the store, please."

Brock reached up and rubbed his forehead. But Summer was giving him a smile so brilliant that he couldn't help but smile, too.

He still loved rules, plans, and things going according to plans. But her spontaneity was growing on him just a little bit. It was adding something to his life that he'd never known he was missing.

Before long, they were back to walking down the sidewalk, pushing their carts overflowing with an abundance of pool noodles and carrying a Best Dressed bag filled with Summer's Welcome Center polo and jeans, with Summer wearing a fluffy yellow ball gown and a smile as bright as the sun.

Okay, he could see that everything to do with this ball gown was in reaction to him being too rigid.

Noted.

Chapter Seven

Summer had walked through the gap in the half wall that separated the Welcome Center offices from the Admissions offices and was sitting in a chair next to Avery's desk. A student had come in for a campus tour earlier and had some unusual admissions questions since they were currently a foreign exchange student, and Summer told her that she'd look into them. And, of course, Avery had all the answers and even typed them up in an email for her.

"We hosted a foreign exchange student once," Avery said.

"Oh yeah?"

Avery nodded. "Nikolas Servais. He was from Belgium."

"Look at how dreamily you said his name!"

"I had such a crush on him back then. We still keep in touch, but I haven't chatted with him in a while. He really was the sweetest boy. Still is. I'm pretty sure he has a girlfriend now, but he said that his grandpa has small flats in both Bruges and Brussels that he only uses for when he's there on business once or twice a month, and that I could stay there if I visited and he'd show me around."

"That *is* super sweet! You should take him up on it."

But Avery turned back to her work, needlessly organizing the things on her desk. "It's too far. And I haven't actually seen him in years."

"So? If he's so sweet, that won't matter."

Avery just shrugged.

A timer sounded on Summer's phone and she smiled, turning it off and going into her texting app. "I was shopping with Brock for some supplies for Aquamoose Tracks on Monday, and he was being his usual rule-follower self and said I shouldn't buy a ball gown we saw in Best Dressed's window because I didn't have anywhere to wear it."

Avery gave an exaggerated gasp and joked, "Doesn't he know you well enough to know you don't like being told what to do?"

"Right? So I bought it, obviously, and I've taken pictures of me wearing it to do ordinary things—going grocery shopping, going for a jog alongside the lake, taking my car to get an oil change, standing in line at Bald Man

Subs, having a game night with friends. I've got something like fifteen different pictures.

"Anyway, I've been setting a timer to go off every two hours so that I can send him another picture of me wearing the dress that he said I couldn't wear anywhere. The one I'm sending now is of me wearing it under the fairy lights at the tri-town meet-up on Wednesday night at Lake Baldwin. I made sure to get lots of people wearing shorts and tank tops in the background."

Avery's laugh was loud enough that everyone in Admissions turned in her direction and smiled. Deja even stood up from her desk across the half wall to see what Avery was laughing at.

Summer raised herself from the chair just enough to see over the half wall to peek at Brock through the glass of his office. He nudged up those dark-framed glasses, then picked up his phone as her text came in. She saw the smile on his face as he opened her text and it made her smile. He just looked at it for a moment, then he touched the screen and started typing a message. She watched as he typed, then sat back down in her chair before he could get a chance to glance up and see her.

Then her phone dinged and she went into the text from Brock.

BROCK: I was obviously wrong when I guessed

how many places you could wear that dress. I stand corrected.

Summer: I'm always willing to help you stand corrected.

She smiled as she put her phone back in her pocket, and couldn't wait until her timer went off again in two hours.

Then Avery sighed. "I have no excitement in my life."

"You should come to a tri-town meet-up with me and Valeria. They're every Wednesday and Saturday and they're fun."

"I can't this week. Maybe next Saturday."

"I'm going to hold you to that." Summer looked around to make sure none of the dozen nearby student employees that Avery managed were close enough to hear. "Pavani is twelve days into recovery and she's dying from boredom. Brock and I are in a competition to see who is going to put on the best presentation at Aquamoose Tracks, and I figure I need to do some research on my competition. So Pavani and I are going to sneak in here late tonight and see what we can dig up. Want to join us?"

Avery squealed and immediately put her hands over her mouth, eyes wide, probably worried that she just gave them away. Summer wasn't sure she'd ever seen anyone so excited about joining her for a little adventure.

"Okay, meet us in the faculty parking lot tonight at eleven."

———

AS SHE STOOD WAITING under the street light in the faculty parking lot, Summer smiled when Pavani and Avery got out of their cars, both dressed in black clothes from head to toe. They both had their hair pulled back in ponytails, and Pavani was even wearing something that looked like a tool belt for someone in Special Ops. Avery held something in her hand that looked like it might be a black beanie. Tonight was going to be fun.

"And you're sure you've recovered enough for this?" Summer asked Pavani.

"I am feeling pretty great, actually!" She lifted her shirt to show an ace bandage wrapping her torso. "My hubby put this around me, though, mostly so I would be reminded that I'm not one hundred percent yet and to not do anything too crazy. Isn't he the cutest thing ever?"

Pavani and Avery didn't seem to want to walk along the sidewalks leading to the Student Center like normal people. So, Summer led them as they snuck around in the shadows, hugging the sides of buildings that were away from the copious lights keeping the campus safe even at night, scurrying between buildings, talking in whispers, always checking for anyone out wandering in the dark.

"Can you just imagine how much Brock would *not* be doing this?" Pavani whispered. "I'm sure this breaks about a million rules."

Summer chuckled just thinking of him doing something like this. They probably weren't breaking any rules at all, but bringing that up wasn't going to give Pavani and Avery the adventure they seemed to desperately need.

They walked past the light just in front of the Arnold Leadership building as quickly as she dared lead Pavani, which wasn't very fast at all, then stopped in a dark nook just beside the main doors. "So," Avery said, "what's going on between you and Brock?"

"What? Nothing."

"She's lying," Pavani whispered. "Don't trust anything she says."

Summer peeked out and saw a campus security guard's back as he walked down the sidewalk they'd need to cross, so they were stuck for a minute. "Okay, I'll share some truth. Neither of us has acknowledged anything. But...I don't know. I've just been noticing lately how good-looking and adorable and sweet and crazy smart he is. And maybe, when we're together working on Aquamoose Tracks together, there's a spark. And when he moves in close, it's a full-on electric charge.

"And I can tell he's feeling it, too. And ladies, he has the most incredible scent. Every time I get close enough to breathe in the goodness, I try to figure out what it is, but I can't. It's clean and crisp and masculine all at the same time and ..." She closed her eyes and relived the scent. "...amazing."

"You are so gone for him, girl," Avery said.

Summer glanced back out at their path, then turned back to her friends. "Maybe. I don't know. But I'm not going to date him because we are coworkers and that's reason enough not to right there."

"Well, that," Pavani whispered to Avery, "and the fact that she's scared."

"No way. Summer isn't afraid of anything."

Summer smiled. She liked when people thought she was fearless. She liked when she felt like she was fearless herself.

Pavani put a hand on Avery's shoulder. "I hate to ruin the vision you've got of Summer, but a girl doesn't go on as many dates as Summer does yet gets to be twenty-seven years old without having had a single serious relationship."

Avery turned her attention to Summer. "None?"

Summer shook her head. "But it's not about fear. I can't even commit on a Thursday to what I'm doing on a Saturday because a better option might come along. A commitment as big as a serious relationship requires is just too hard to even comprehend. The coast is clear. Let's go!"

As they hurried from the leadership building to the Clark Geoscience building, a deep voice called out, "Hey!"

All three of them froze right where they stood, and they turned their heads to see a campus security guard walking in their direction from a couple dozen feet away. How had she missed him when she'd peeked out to check if the coast was clear?

"Fudge buckets!" Avery hissed.

"What are you three up to this late at night?" The officer stopped a good fifteen feet away, shining his flashlight between all three of them, who just happened to look about as guilty as could be. Then he said, "Summer Graham?"

Summer stood up straight. "Mike Gunnell?" Then she turned to Avery and Pavani and whispered, "I'm going to distract him. As soon as he's not looking, you book it the rest of the way to the Student Center. I'll find a way to catch up with you there."

They both nodded affirmation like she was their squad leader, and she walked up to Mike, making sure she stood so that he had to turn his attention away from Avery and Pavani to talk to her. "Hi! It's so good to see you! How's Olivia?"

"Getting so big! She'll be nine months old next week. The bigger question is why are you all sneaking? You know your access badge is always active until midnight, right?"

"Yeah, but Pavani and Avery need a little adventure in their lives. Want to help?"

He nodded like he totally understood that need, and they both turned to look at Avery and Pavani as they scurried alongside a building, half-crouching, half-running toward the Student Center. "You bet I do."

"Okay, give us five minutes, then come to the Student Center and shine your flashlight through the glass to the Welcome Center lobby. I'll keep the door to the offices open when we get there, so make sure you shine the light back that direction, too."

The guard nodded, arms folded, a big grin on his face.

"That'll be our cue to hide. Your access badge will open the Welcome Center door, right?" He nodded, so she continued. "Okay, then come in and shine your flashlight around the offices, but don't find us. And Mike? There aren't good hiding places, so it's going to be really hard not to find us. And Pavani is under doctor's orders to not do anything too crazy." She probably should've found a way to keep Pavani from doing the crouch-run thing she was currently doing. If that was even possible with Pavani.

Mike reached a fist out in her direction, so she bumped it with hers.

"Thanks, Mike."

"Anytime. I needed a little something to keep me awake and alert tonight."

When Summer got to the doors of the Student Center, she didn't see Pavani and Avery and worried that they might have had a bit of a communication error until the two women stepped out from where they were hiding behind the bushes beside the door. "Sneaky."

She used her access badge to open the doors, and then they snuck down the hallway, hugging the walls, like that would somehow make them invisible, as they walked toward the doors to the Welcome Center. Then Summer used her access badge to open that door, too, then the door to the offices.

In no time at all, they were all standing inside of Brock's office, marveling at the sparse, clean, tidy space.

"They've already emptied his garbage," Avery said, "so no clues there. Maybe he keeps notes in his files." She walked to the filing drawer he had at the side of his desk and crouched down to pull it open. She started rifling through the tabbed items.

"Nah," Pavani said. "He probably keeps it in files on his computer. Do you want me to hack into it?"

"Do you even know how to hack into a computer?" Summer asked.

"No, but I can guess passwords as good as anyone else. It's probably something like ILik3Rul3s or p3rf3ctionist or maybe even LusciousH@ir because he really does have luscious hair." She jiggled his mouse to bring the screen to life.

But Summer wasn't looking at her friends. She had found a sheet of long, skinny notepaper sitting in the middle of Brock's desk, with his perfectly neat handwriting with the strong, sharp corners and perfectly straight lines. The paper said *Thursday* at the top, then had everything listed that he planned to get done that day. And the list was *long*. Even if someone was perfectly efficient, she didn't think they could get so many things done in a day. Why in the world did he expect so much of himself?

She started scanning the list. Some of the items were boring things, like remembering to email or call someone or to research something related to some type of scholarship. A few were meetings he had with people in the office or with local businesses or with prospective or current students. And, of course, he had included his meeting with her tomorrow afternoon. And she swore that his handwriting on that item was different from the others. A bit more curved than angled. Softer.

Then her eyes fell to the next item on the list: *Find a way to tell Summer how beautiful she looks in every ball gown picture she sends me.*

There was a moment when her insides melted and she was seeing hearts floating all around her. And then came the feeling of wrongness—that what they were doing was invasive. She never guessed they would actually find something personal in his office. She set the to-do list back down where it had been. "We need to get out of here."

Just then, Mike's flashlight shone into the Welcome

Center lobby and Avery yelped. "Oh, shiitake mushrooms, we're going to get caught!"

Summer rushed them out of Brock's office and shut the door behind them. "Avery, hide under Deja's desk. Pavani, you get between the ficus and that filing cabinet and be careful with yourself or Zain is never going to trust me with you again." They scurried into their spots, and Summer hid behind one of the padded chairs in the common area, right by where they had their morning stand-ups. It was about the worst place she'd hidden in her life.

A moment later, she heard the Welcome Center door open, and Mike's voice call out, "Is anyone in here? I better not find anyone here, or you're probably going to get arrested or something."

She heard Avery gasp, so she peeked around the chair to where her friend was hiding to see if she was okay. A look of exhilaration filled Avery's whole face. Her whole body, actually. Yeah, she wasn't scared. Summer smiled as she pulled her head back and Mike's flashlight shone haphazardly around the area.

Then there was a second voice. "Oh, Mike. I'm glad you got here quickly. I just saw on the monitors some kids sneak in here. Have you found them?"

Mike laughed nervously. "Kids? Nah. There are no kids in here."

True.

"I saw them."

"Then they're gone now. Come on; let's get this place locked up."

Summer peeked out to see Mike's hand on the other campus security guard's shoulder, trying to get him to turn toward the door.

"Not until I'm confident that we've fully checked out the place."

———

PAVANI AND AVERY looked every bit as chagrined as Summer felt as the three of them sat on the hard chairs in the Campus Security office while Officer Hauber ran their access cards through their security system.

Then he turned around. "Want to explain to me why the three of you were hiding in a place that you have clearance to be in?"

"Not really," Summer said. It wasn't like she could come up with a reason that wouldn't sound totally stupid.

But Officer Hauber just stood, feet shoulder-width apart, arms crossed, looking like he wasn't going anywhere until he got answers.

Avery was the first one to break. She pointed at Summer and said, "We're here because Summer has a crush on a boy we work with!"

Summer's face immediately heated up. They were going to start calling her Sunburn instead of Summer.

But apparently, that was a good enough reason for the security guard. He put a hand over his eyes and shook his head, but then told them they were free to go.

They weren't exactly there because she had a crush on a boy.

But then again, maybe it was time that she admitted to herself that they really kind of were.

Chapter Eight

BROCK

Brock's arms were full with all the cards, pamphlets, and booklets for the Aquamoose Tracks packets that he'd just picked up from the campus printer, so he was glad that Avery was headed into the Welcome Center at the same time as him and could grab the door.

"Thanks," he said as he walked past her. She dropped her gaze like she was feeling awkward being around him, which made no sense. So he asked, "What brings you to the Welcome Center side of the wall?" just to make small talk.

"I'm looking for Summer."

She was headed toward the door that led to their offices, so he said, "Come with me. I'm pretty sure she's in the meeting room with the ambassadors." He nudged his glasses back up with his shoulder. They both headed down the other hallway and sure enough, Summer was sitting on the table at the front of the room, her five Friday afternoon ambassadors seated in the front row of chairs.

"Oh! Good!" she said, seeing what Brock carried. "I was hoping those would be ready." Then her eyes went to Avery, along with everyone else's.

Avery didn't seem to like all the attention, and she ducked her chin and tucked a lock of hair behind her ear. "I didn't mean to interrupt. I just came to say thank you for inviting me last night, Summer. I haven't had that much fun in a long time."

"I'm glad you came." Summer gave her a smile back that seemed equal parts happy for Avery and like it held a secret that they both shared. Summer's eyes met Brock's for a brief second, but then they dropped to the floor, just like Avery's had after meeting his eyes earlier, and he wondered again what was going on. But then Summer's eyes went back to the group of ambassadors, Avery ducked out of the room, and Summer clapped her hands once, getting everyone's attention back on her.

"Okay, we've got a big enough group scheduled for campus tours this afternoon that we'll need three tour guides. Haley, Rhett, and Misaki, you're up. Paige and Nia, you'll be at the Welcome Center front desk, and you'll get to work on putting all those packets together." She held her arms out toward the huge stack of printed goods that Brock held like she was showing off their prize.

As Nia and Paige headed up to the lobby, their arms laden with the printed goods Brock had handed off to them, Summer turned to the other three ambassadors. "Elle is going to run the group session today. If you need me for anything, I'll be in the staging area with Brock, getting things prepped for our first Aquamoose Tracks of the school year. It's next Friday! Are you guys excited?"

The three of them cheered, and Summer waved at them as Elle came into the room and she and Brock headed out.

As soon as they got into the staging area, Brock said, "I know you're excited for this, but do you think we'll actually be ready in time? We both have pretty busy weeks with non-Aquamoose Tracks responsibilities."

She put a hand on his shoulder and looked right into his eyes, sending a thrill right through him. "We're going to be ready in time. We've got this. This is my fourth '*First* Aquamoose Tracks of the new school year' I've planned. The sixteenth I've planned total. If you add the ones I helped with in different capacities as an ambassador, it's another thirty on top of that. So I can tell you from experience that everything is awesome, and it's going to go great."

He smiled, honestly a bit relieved, and looked at the schedule in his hand.

"So, of course, things are going to go wrong."

He looked up at her in alarm, and she laughed.

"Brock, things *always* go wrong. It's a huge event with so many moving parts, it's to be expected. But those things are going to work out fine in the end, too."

Part of him believed her. But the other part really just believed that if things went wrong, then that meant that he hadn't planned well enough or executed things well enough.

"Come in close. Let's send Pavani an update."

He scooted in next to her as she unlocked her phone. Instead of clicking on the camera, she went straight into her texting app and chose Pavani's name. Since he was standing right next to Summer, before she clicked on the camera icon, he saw that the last text she'd received from Pavani said, *Thank you SOOOOO much for last night! When I got home, I slept for 12 hours straight. Best sleep I've ever gotten. You cured two weeks' worth of cabin fever in 82 minutes flat.*

He looked at Summer. "Wow—you've gotten enthusiastic thank yous for last night from both Pavani and Avery. What did you guys do?"

Summer shrugged. "Just an evening of girl stuff." The smile she gave made him wonder even more what it had been all about. She took a picture of the two of them, making sure to get as much of the ever-expanding supplies that were filling the room in the frame. Then she typed something quickly that he didn't see and sent off the picture.

He pulled out the schedule, and they started going through each thing one at a time, making sure they had all the supplies they needed for each one. They had only gotten to the second item when Tess popped her head into the room.

"Summer, will you come see me in my office after you two finish up here? I want to talk with you about an email I got from campus security about the incident with you, Pavani, and Avery last night."

When Tess ducked back out of the staging room, Brock set the schedule on the long counter that ran along one side of the room and turned to Summer, an eyebrow raised. "Your 'evening of girl stuff' included an incident with campus security?"

She looked unabashed and lifted one shoulder. "Sometimes, a girl's got to live on the edge."

Was it wrong that he was so attracted to her right now?

Yes, it was wrong. He liked when people followed the rules and did what they were supposed to do in the best possible way they could do it.

Except he was *very* attracted to her. More and more so as they got closer to pulling off Aquamoose Tracks. And being attracted to her was a very bad idea. He picked up the schedule again and moved on to the third item on the list, and then the fourth.

"You already have the schedule of which ambassadors will be leading groups on the campus tours, right?"

Summer nodded. "I'll add it to the shared spreadsheet when I get back to my desk. Let's take a look at the host assignments and make sure we haven't missed anything." A moment after they both leaned over the complicated spreadsheet, Summer stood up straight, pulled her phone out of her pocket, and looked at the screen. "Oh, it's my dad 'popping onto your phone to tell you I love you.' Hang on." She typed a message in return, then pushed the phone back into her pocket.

He glanced over at her as she leaned in to look at their legal-sized paper. "That's sweet. You two are pretty close, right?"

She seemed to consider her answer for a bit before she said, "Our relationship is kind of complicated. But he loves me and I love him, so I guess that part's not so complicated. He was just never around enough when I was growing up, you know?"

"What about your mom? Are your parents still married?"

"They are. That relationship is a bit more complicated. But I guess it's also uncomplicated in that they still love each other enough to put up with each other."

She didn't seem to want to say more, so he didn't

press. She used her finger to follow a line across, and then tapped a part at the bottom like it confirmed what she was checking. "What about your family?"

He looked up, pushed his glasses back to their right spot, and tried to think of a good way to describe his family. "Okay, picture a family with a mom and a dad and two kids sitting down in a pristine house to a home-cooked family dinner where everyone is perfectly behaved, and they always say 'please' and 'thank you' and 'may I be excused' at the end of the meal." He glanced at Summer and she nodded like it was exactly what she expected his family to be like. "Okay, now imagine the exact opposite of that, and more than double the number of kids. That's my family."

Summer laughed a boisterous laugh. It wasn't the first time he'd heard her laugh like that, but it was the first time he'd been the one to cause it. The feeling spreading through his chest made him want to cause her to laugh like that again soon.

"We mostly just annoyed each other a lot. Do you have any siblings?" She shook her head. "Well, sometimes we annoyed each other for sport because that's what siblings do." He smiled just thinking about it. "Other times, it was just because there were five of us and it was kind of inevitable. But no matter how much we annoyed each other, we still loved each other unconditionally. We are much better friends as adults, and I'm very grateful for that. Family is important."

Her eyes stayed on him for a long moment, studying him. Then she looked down at the spreadsheet, but he got the impression that she wasn't seeing the words on it at all. He looked down at the spreadsheet too and stayed quiet, not quite knowing what he was supposed to do. After a moment, he felt like maybe she had something she wanted to say but needed a nudge. He tried to think of how to give her that nudge.

"I take it your family wasn't like that?"

It seemed like a long time before she spoke again. Then she cleared her throat and her voice came out in a hushed quiet. "I was six, and my mom was in a funk, which, for her, meant drinking a lot of wine. I usually just played by myself in my toy room when she was like that, but for whatever reason—probably because I wanted the company—I was playing on the floor next to her in her study. I guess the wine made her feel entirely too truthful, and she told me that being a mother wasn't her thing. She just wasn't cut out for it. It was nothing against me and I shouldn't take it person- ally—but it just wasn't for her and she didn't want to do it.

"But how could I not take that personally? I was her only child. It was *obviously* about me. Later, when she was sober, she apologized and said she hadn't meant to tell me that. But she also said that now that the cat was out of the bag, she was going to stop pretending and start living her life.

"I was pretty sure my dad liked being my dad, but he was also gone all the time for work. I think I put all my needs to be loved on my dad's shoulders from that moment on, but even at six, I knew full well that he wasn't capable of being all that I needed. I knew I was largely on my own."

Brock's heart was breaking for Summer, and he desperately wanted to reach out and wrap his arms around her.

She cleared her throat. "That's not a story I share with anyone. *Ever*. Not even with Valeria. When I was a kid, I always made up elaborate excuses about why my mom had to be somewhere else instead of with me. Or sometimes I just said I didn't have a mom. I never told anyone that my mom wasn't there because she just simply didn't want to be my mom. So, please—"

"I won't ever share it with anyone," Brock said. "You have my word. Summer, you need to know that your mom told the truth when she said it wasn't about you. Some people desperately want to be a mother and never get the chance. And some people don't want to be mothers but get the chance anyway. It's not fair, but neither of those situations has anything to do with the child. And I'm here to tell you that your mother not wanting to be a mom had nothing at all to do with you."

Summer swallowed hard and although she didn't cry, her eyes reddened and she sniffed. Then she fanned her face with her hand, like she was trying to dry any tears that were thinking about forming, and said, "I'm sorry. I really didn't mean to bring the mood down."

Brock reached out and, with a finger, he lifted her chin. "You're not responsible for making sure everyone is having fun all the time. You're allowed to feel your feelings."

He held her chin, and she held his gaze, and they both stood there, an understanding passing between them, a connection forged through vulnerability that hadn't been there before.

"I've got updated numbers on our first Aquamoose Tracks!" Everett had started talking before he was fully in the room, and he froze as soon as he saw them.

Brock quickly dropped his hand and turned toward his coworker.

"I'm sorry. Is this a bad time?"

Summer shook her head and forced a smile. She cut a quick glance at Brock—a silent acknowledgment that she was pushing her feelings away instead of feeling them— and said, "Nope, it's great. What do you have for us?"

Everett smiled big. "The September event just sold out."

"Oh, that's fantastic!" Summer said.

"Since Moose on the Loose is such a favorite high

school hangout, I asked if they would send an email to their list about the event, and they said they were happy to help *and* they offered to put up signs in all five of their cafes. Four hours later, we had filled the last dozen spots. The October, November, and January events got a big boost in numbers, too."

"That's really great, man," Brock said.

Everett clapped Brock on the shoulder. "We might just meet our applicant goal number by December first after all."

When Everett walked back out of the staging area—probably to share the great news with everyone else in the office—Summer met Brock's eyes. Then she gave him a small smile and said, "Thank you."

He smiled and gave a nod of acknowledgment, then, following Summer's lead, turned back to the schedule and their assessment of things needed, feeling a pull toward Summer that was stronger than he'd ever felt before.

Chapter Nine

SUMMER

*D*eja walked from her desk to the doorway of Summer's office, a paper in her hand. "You don't usually work so late—I can't believe I am beating you out of here."

Summer looked up from the email she was working on and glanced at the other offices—it looked like Brock's office was the only one with the lights on still. She couldn't believe it got so late without her even noticing. "It's been a very full day." She did an event at a high school in Huron, so she had two and a half hours of driving, she had an ambassador come in for coaching, she had to work on next week's ambassador schedule, and had to do a few last-minute things for Aquamoose Tracks.

Then she realized that she really needed to send an email to all the ambassadors before their first Aquamoose

Tracks since all of them would be present. It was sometimes tricky to manage so many different personalities, make sure they all felt like their voices were heard, and maintain a good group culture.

"I just wanted to confirm"—Deja held up the paper in her hand—"you want me to put in an order for six pairs of moose slippers, right?"

Summer smiled. "Yes. It's for a relay race—I want to switch things up when I visit high schools."

Deja chuckled. "Okay, then, you do you. I just wanted to make sure I wasn't reading it wrong. Hey, I haven't heard you say boo about your dates for the past few weeks. Have you not been dating or have you just been keeping your mouth shut about it? Because hearing all about them is like a possum eatin' a sweet tater to some of us."

"Oh, you know I'd tell you all about them. I've just been busy lately." Summer was never too busy for dating— that was something she would always make time for. The truth was that she hadn't been as interested in dating ever since her thoughts started focusing themselves in Brock's direction lately. It was probably a bad thing, but she couldn't quite convince herself to stop thinking of him.

"Nope, nope, nope," Deja said, shaking her head. "Don't allow yourself to get too busy to stay on the lookout for the one! Having a large base of friends is amazing, but it's nothing compared to having a partner in life."

Deja's words weren't so different from sentiments

she'd heard the woman say many times over their years working together, but this time, they hit her in a way they hadn't before. "How did you get to be so smart?"

"Girl, I was born being right about everything. It's right there in my name—Deja Wright. 'Deja' means again, so my name literally means 'Right, again.'"

Summer couldn't hold back her smile. "Is that why you married Trent—so you could gain a last name that would encapsulate you?"

Deja held up a finger. "I married him for his last name *and* because he's a fine hunk of man, *and* because I constantly just want to grab him with both hands and kiss his face like it's made of sugar, *and* because I enjoy a stroll hand-in-hand with him along the shore of Lake Baldwin, *and* to face anything in life that tries to whup us, *and* do it side-by-side. Every single bit of all of it."

"*Aww,*" Summer said, "that's so sweet!" And she wasn't just saying that—it did sound sweet.

Deja looked at the paper in her hand for a moment. Not like she was reading anything on it, but like she was trying to decide whether to say something. She apparently decided yes, which, knowing Deja, was kind of inevitable. "I know you want a family and kids someday. Do you ever think about why you never have serious relationships, even though plenty of guys you've gone on dates with have seemed to really want that?"

Summer shrugged. "Not really." Okay, it was somewhat a lie. She had thought about it, then quickly started thinking about other things.

"Well, honey, maybe it's time that you start to wonder if it's because you just haven't met the right guy yet—and if that's the case, you keep doing what you're doing. If it's not that, then maybe it's time to wonder if you're afraid of commitment."

"I might not like commitment, Deja, but I'm not afraid of it."

Deja held her gaze for a long moment, then gave a quick nod. "Okay, then, good to hear. Now, I'm going to get home to my man. Don't stay too late, you hear?"

"I won't."

Summer was finishing up her email when she got a text from Valeria.

VALERIA: Don't hate me, but I have to cancel tonight. My mamá called and said that my abuela is having a rough day and apparently I'm the only one she remembers today, or at least the only one she trusts today, and she won't stop asking for me. So I'm going to have to drive to Sunrise to spend the evening with her. I'm sad to miss out on our girls' night!

SUMMER: [three crying-faced emojis] You know I

could never hate you! Go be with your abuela— make her smile that smile she only gives you.

Summer put down her phone, sent the email, shut down her laptop, and let out a big sigh. Now, what was she going to do tonight? She and Valeria had planned their girls' night for tonight precisely because nothing was going on with their friend group or at the lake or at the college. She couldn't even call her dad to chat because he was at a work event.

She could just go have a quiet night alone at her apartment.

Yeah, like she was going to hang out alone with her thoughts about whether her life was headed in the right direction and if she was going to still be single five or ten years from now, and then wonder if she was ever going to have that family of her own that she wanted.

No, thank you. She needed people. Maybe Brock was right and she did deserve to feel whatever feelings she had. But that didn't mean that she *wanted* to.

She looked through the glass front of her office and across the common area to where she could see part of Brock through the glass front of his office. Before she let herself think about whether it was a wise idea or not, she stood up, grabbed her purse, turned her office lights off, pulled her door shut, and walked straight over to Brock's office.

"Hi." She was a pro at dating and flirting, yet "hi" was all her brain came up with.

He looked up at her and smiled big enough that it lifted his glasses just a bit, and it made her entire insides warm. "Hello."

"Are you doing anything tonight? Or do you want to?"

"As long as it includes getting food, yes. I'm starving."

Thirty minutes later, they were sitting in a booth at a cute Indian restaurant in Golden Springs that Summer didn't go to nearly often enough, eating naan bread under a dimmed light, the scents of simmering curry and turmeric surrounding them.

And the warm light hanging just over their table flickered every once in a while, making it feel sort of like candlelight and cast the most amazing glow on Brock. She was glad it was just the two of them at dinner because then she could gaze at him all she wanted as they chatted and it would just seem like she was present and attentive.

They both reached out for a vegetable samosa at the same time, and their hands brushed before Brock pulled his back, motioning for her to go first. But she didn't want his hand pulled out of the way. She wanted it back where it was, so she could see if the slight touch still held the same zing after it had been touching hers for more than a quick second. Like maybe all night.

"So," Summer said, "have you started having the pre-Aquamoose Tracks nightmares yet?"

"That's a thing?"

She nodded. "Every single time. This morning, I dreamt that I was trying to talk about the schedule in the session with the parents and prospective students, but I was wearing the Aquamoose mascot costume, and no one could hear me through the giant moose headpiece. I wanted to take it off, but I kept tripping over my scaled feet every time I tried."

Brock laughed his amused chuckle, and it suddenly made everything feel peaceful and right. "Last night, for me, I kept forgetting where I set the schedule down and I couldn't remember what was on it, but I didn't want anyone to know I misplaced it. So I kept making up things and sending students and ambassadors in all the wrong places and doing all the wrong things and then the place was like a circus. Two nights ago, I dreamed that we got hit by a tsunami right in the middle of our presentations, causing a massive flood. And the tsunami came from Lake Baldwin."

Summer laughed out loud. "Well, it seems the worst-case scenarios have already happened, so all that's left is for the event to go well, right?"

"Yes. Let's go with that plan."

Their waiter came and set each of their entrees down in front of them, the scent of chicken coconut korma wafting up from Summer's plate. She breathed in deeply, then took a bite, unable to wait any longer to get the taste in her mouth.

"Did you know that brains burn more calories when thinking hard than when they're doing less cognitive-intense things?"

"Huh," Brock said. "That explains why I'm so hungry. I spent hours working with Johanna in Financial Aid, figuring out whether the academic scholarship budget is going to stretch far enough to cover all of our applicants this year. How about your day? Was it extra mentally taxing?"

She loaded up another bite on her fork. "It was long, but nope—I just *really* like Indian food." And then she stuck the forkful of curry goodness in her mouth as Brock chuckled.

As she watched him use his fork and knife to perfectly cut up each piece of meat and every vegetable on his plate, she couldn't help but imagine what he had been like when he was younger, before they started working together. Especially when he was in high school, since they both worked with so many students who were that age. "What was high school like for you?"

He stopped and thought for a minute, then said, "My hobbies in high school included striving for straight A's, playing basketball with friends, and worrying too much. What about you?"

That sounded about right. "Mine...Let's see." She tried

to encapsulate high school with three things. "I guess my hobbies included hanging out with friends, trying to experience all of life at once, and rebelling against things my dad thought were important."

Brock's eyebrow rose. "You rebelled against your dad? Not your mom?"

"Yeah," Summer said with a shrug. "I don't know what psychiatrists would have to say about that, but what my mom wanted me to do or not do was irrelevant. It was all about my dad.

"I never rebelled big, though. It wasn't like I started using drugs or alcohol or decided to become a vagabond and forget college or anything like that. It was little things. Like my dad said it was important to eat a healthy breakfast, so I'd eat a donut. He said posture was important and got me a nice desk with an ergonomic chair for doing homework, so I did it on my bed. He said I had to do homework before I went out with friends in the evening, so I just pretended that I did it but really watched YouTube videos, then did my homework at eleven p.m. when I got home."

"Ahh. A rebel who still gets her homework done."

"Well, good grades were important to *me*." She paused for a moment. "And now that I look back on my rebelling, I realize that all the things that were important to him were things that were good for me. So I guess one of my hobbies in high school was making stupid choices. Because there was more than one time that I woke up in the morning with a page of my math textbook stuck to my face or the metal coil of a notebook imprinted on my cheek."

Brock laughed, and she soaked in the way he laughed when they were in public. It was a mix between a boisterous laugh and a restrained laugh that she wasn't sure she'd ever seen another person pull off.

Summer took another bite of her korma, savored it as she chewed, then swallowed and motioned to Brock with her fork. "Okay, so I shared something embarrassing from my childhood last week. I think that means you have to share something from yours."

"Something that scarred me for life, preferably?"

Summer laughed. "Preferably."

He looked upward, thinking for a minute, then said, "Okay, okay, I've got one. I'll go with a story from when I was the same age as you were in your story. I'm the oldest. My siblings are all close together in age, but there's a four year gap between me and them. So my mom relied on me a lot to help, especially because I had a lot of younger siblings. So this one time, I was six, my twin sisters were two, my brother was one, and my mom was in the house getting my baby brother down for a nap.

"We were all in the backyard, and I was pushing one sister in the swing. My other sister and my brother were digging with sticks in the dirt. But what none of us knew was that what they were digging at was a mud wasp hole, and they made them super angry."

Summer's hand flew over her mouth. "Oh no!"

"Yeah, so they came out and started stinging my brother and sister and they were screaming, so my other sister and I started screaming, too. I pulled my sister out of the swing, picked up my little brother, grabbed my other sister's hand, and we all ran in the house screaming, angry wasps following us most of the way, stinging us as we went. We burst into the house, and my littlest brother woke up—of course—and started screaming, too."

"Anyway, everything was chaotic as my mom took care of our stings, but *I* was the one who got into trouble because I should've been watching my brother and sister better and not let that happen." He turned his palms up and shrugged. "And thus goes the curse of the oldest child."

Summer leaned back in her chair. "Ahh. This explains so much."

"It does? Oh, no. Did I give you too much material to analyze me with?"

Summer tried to hide a smile.

"Let me guess—you're going to say that I learned that others can mess up, but I can't. *I* need to be perfect."

"Ahh, interesting," she said, nodding at his self-assessment. "Your analysis explains a lot, too."

He rubbed the back of his neck. "That's not what you were going to say?"

"I was going to say that you think you should have the ability to control the uncontrollable. You know, like thinking that an event with one hundred fifty students, plus their parents, plus fifty ambassadors, that went overnight, traipsed all over the campus, included lots of activities, and required feeding and housing would all go one hundred percent according to plan. That's impossible. There are a lot of factors that aren't controllable. People are unpredictable. And sometimes there are wasps you don't know about."

Brock shook his head, chuckling. "Okay, you got me there. But I still believe that you can up your chances of it going according to plan by being as prepared as possible."

"And I agree. To a certain extent, because it does get to a point where you're not getting the same return on investment."

"If you're getting *any* return on investment, it's worth it."

They were just going to have to agree to disagree on that one.

As the waiter came and took away their plates as they finished, Summer said, "Okay, I've got another question for you. If time, money, and responsibilities weren't a factor, what would you be doing?"

"Hmm. You go first—I need more time to think about my answer."

"Fair enough. Okay, mine's easy. I want to experience everything there is to experience. Travel to all the places. Try all the things. But I want to do all that with a big group of fun people. So if money wasn't a factor, I would choose to pay for all of them to be able to experience all the things with me." It wasn't even one of those "wouldn't it be nice?" dreams—it was an actual goal of hers.

Brock smiled, but she wasn't sure if he was just smiling because he had guessed her answer, or if it was because it sounded like a fun thing to him, too.

"What about you? What would you do?"

Brock wiped his napkin across his mouth and put it on the table. "College made a huge difference in my life. You know how when you're growing up, you think that the way your family does things is normal and that it's the one and only way to do things?"

Summer nodded.

"I grew up in Golden Springs, so Lake Baldwin University was only a twenty minute drive away. But I got enough scholarship money to live on campus, and that made all the difference to me. It helped me to, I don't know, find myself. To realize that there are other ways of doing things, and some of those ways were better. I know I have an issue with perfectionism, but some of the ways I did things were setting me up for failure, no matter how hard I tried to be perfect at them. Living away from home during college was life-changing for me.

"So, I guess if I could do anything, it would be exactly what I'm doing. Helping other kids to experience something different from what they'd experienced their whole lives, so they can see with fresh eyes which of the things they've always done is working for them and which things aren't."

Summer just gazed at the man across the table, a new appreciation for him forming so much more concretely in her head. It made her want to reach a hand across the table and hold his. To go walk along the shore of Lake Baldwin with him and talk late into the night. To do all the things Deja said was wonderful about having a partner for life.

She allowed herself to reach across the table and give his hand a squeeze, ignoring how right it felt, and said, "You're a good man, Brock." And then she ignored how he turned his hand to squeeze hers back and the look he was giving her as he gazed into her eyes. She didn't even allow herself the chance to interpret what the look meant because everything was definitely heading into the danger zone. She glanced out across the dining room for their waiter. "I guess it's time to pay the bill and head home."

She also ignored the look of disappointment on Brock's face when she suggested they end the night.

Summer didn't fear change. Change was exciting. There was always something else great on the horizon, so she never felt like she had to hold on to the past. It made it easy for her to take risks.

Except when it came to work.

As ephemeral as she could handle anything else in her life being—in fact, everything else changing was something she generally sought out—the Welcome Center was always the one constant. The people there had been her family for nine years. She wasn't about to do anything to risk that. And falling as completely for Brock that she was feeling like she could easily fall for him would definitely risk things at work.

Chapter Ten

BROCK

The Aquamoose Tracks excitement in the room was so palpable that Brock felt like he could reach out and touch it. The ballroom was filled with one hundred and fifty prospective students, most with a parent or two, all seated and going through the packet of information they got at the door, chatting with each other as they waited for the event to start.

A child, probably not more than four years old, was at the back of the ballroom, which was kind of strange. Kids weren't really allowed at this event, so he figured the little girl's parent must've gotten special permission. She had a purple helium balloon tied to her wrist, and she was dancing around, making the balloon bounce with every move.

Summer leaned in from where they both stood at the

front of the room, just beside the stage. "Isn't this amazing?"

"It really is." He'd worked in the Welcome Center for the past four years, so he'd helped out at this event a lot. They all had. But he'd never been co-in charge of it before, and it made everything so different. There was a nervous anticipation, sure, but an even stronger excitement as they watched everything that they had planned for happen in real time. "Good luck up there."

Summer walked up the steps onto the stage and welcomed everyone. She was such a natural. It was like she was being energized just by being in front of that many people.

How had he never noticed how incredible she was on stage before? He'd always thought she did a good job and that she was the best person to be over this event. But it had never hit him before how amazing she was at getting such a huge crowd excited and pumped up to sit and listen to people talk.

And then, as she was talking to the crowd and connecting with them, he couldn't help but think—again— about their dinner earlier in the week and how she'd ended the night so quickly. He'd been just about to ask her if she wanted to take a walk down Main Street or something so they could keep talking. They had been connecting on a level that he hadn't connected with anyone in a very long time. Possibly ever. All he knew was that he felt differently about her than he had about anyone else he'd ever dated.

But he wasn't sure how she felt about him. Since their dinner Monday night, she'd been friendly at work, but she was definitely not pushing to make their relationship move beyond anything other than coworkers. He'd kind of thought she was interested, though, because their hands had accidentally brushed a few more times, and it seemed like it had affected her just as much as it had affected him.

After introducing the event, Summer was the moderator of a rotating panel—they had a representative from each school or college at the university come up to the podium and talk about the degree programs under their umbrella—and she made sure none of them went longer than their allotted three minutes.

Then, before he knew it, Summer was introducing him and inviting him to come up on stage and talk about scholarships. There was a buzzing in his stomach that he was pretty sure wasn't nerves, which was what he'd anticipated feeling. Excitement, maybe? That was probably it— it was something he hadn't guessed but probably should have. He'd be doing his favorite part of the job, and he'd be reaching so many people while he did it.

"You've got this," Summer said as he stepped onto the stage, right before she stepped down off it, handing it all over to him.

He was glad that in the "who could give the best

presentation" competition with Summer he got to go first. This whole event was packed with a lot of information, and he wanted the students and parents to know all about scholarships before they hit overload.

Plus, okay, with as great as Summer was at doing the introduction and moderating, he really didn't want to give his presentation right after Summer gave hers.

He looked out at the crowd of eager faces. "Raise your hand if you've looked online for scholarships before."

Most of the prospective students raised their hands. Good.

"Okay, keep them up if you think it's been a difficult process."

Most kept their hands up, and a lot of kids looked around, seemingly surprised that they weren't the only ones struggling with it. A few nodded or held their hands up with more gusto. He figured as much.

"I'll share a little secret with you. Scholarships available nationally are *not* where people tend to get the money they need for school. And if they do, it's very rare. Most of the scholarships people get are local. A lot from your high school or the college you'll be going to, and some from local businesses.

"It can take a while to find all those, too, but we've made it a lot easier for you. We've scoured the internet to find all the scholarships available specifically for Lake Baldwin State University students. We've also gone to businesses all over the state to see if any of them would be willing to sponsor scholarships for LBSU students."

He paused a moment, just long enough to build a small amount of anticipation. "And then we brought them all together on LBSU's site. Raise your hand if you have already applied to Lake Baldwin State *and* you've already been accepted."

About eight kids raised their hands.

"Okay, now keep your hand up if you've already gotten your Aquamoose ID *and* know your login information."

Most of the hands hesitantly went down until only one remained. He let out a huge breath of relief that at least one hand was still up. His presentation wasn't as awesome if it wasn't with an actual future student.

"How would you like to go home tomorrow knowing that you already applied for scholarships?" He might as well have asked the kid if he wanted to win a laptop by how excited he was. "Come on up."

As the high school senior who introduced himself as Dylan logged into the laptop connected to the big screen, Brock took a moment to really look out at the crowd and saw how engaged everyone was. A few were taking notes. So far, so good. Summer caught his eye and gave him a huge smile.

Once Dylan was logged in and the LBSU scholarship page was on the screen, it showed all the scholarships that he, specifically, was eligible for, based on his school information and declared major.

"Whoa!" the boy said. "There are hundreds! I can apply for all of these?"

Brock nodded. "Back on that first page, there is one three-hundred word essay. It's a global essay for all of them. Some will require other pieces of information, and some will require an additional essay. More than half of them only require you to apply. Now, let me show you the best part. See that checkmark next to each of the scholarships? You can hand pick the ones you want to apply for, then click the 'Apply' button at the top. Want to apply for all of them? Just click the 'select all' option before clicking 'Apply.'"

"And that's it?"

Brock grinned. "For a lot of them, yes. Click on that tab that says 'Follow-up.' That's where you go to see what additional information some of them might need from you."

A ripple of chatting moved through the room. Most of the rest of his presentation came from answering questions while the kid at the laptop clicked around to check out different parts of the site. They had lots of questions, and he even made them laugh a couple of times. When he was done, the applause was enthusiastic and he was smiling pretty big as he stepped off the stage. It had gone pretty well, if he did think so himself.

Summer got up after him, riled up the crowd even more about scholarships, and then went into her presentation. He was so glad that she hadn't gone first, or his would've seemed dull by comparison. She brought so much more excitement; she even had Baldy the Aquamoose—LBSU's mascot—join her presentation.

She started talking about all the social events at the university, and in hearing it, he was actually getting nostalgic about school and wished he was a student again just to re-experience it all. She got the crowd involved and excited and so invested in Lake Baldwin State.

Then she showed a video of students on campus telling about their favorite parts. It would start with the camera on the student, then cut to a video of that exact activity happening, the students' words working as a voice-over.

From the corner of his eye, he noticed something purple and moving, and glanced toward the back of the carpeted ballroom in time to see that the little girl had managed to untie her balloon from her wrist, and it was floating up to the ceiling high above.

Honestly, his only thought had been that it was sad she lost her balloon because it was far too high to reach and would probably stay up there for a few days before drifting back to the ground.

But then the fire alarm sounded, blaring loud and obliterating all other sounds. Almost as one, everyone in the audience brought their hands up to cover their ears. About two seconds after that, the sprinklers in the ceiling turned on, apparently having wrongly assumed that the balloon was smoke and a fire needed to be put out.

Chaos erupted almost immediately. People could've guessed that a fire alarm might be false, but the sprinklers sending water down on all of them seemed to confirm that it wasn't. Quite a few people screamed—whether it was from fear of fire or shock from the rain, it was hard to tell— and everyone stood and made their way toward the doors at the back and side of the room, knocking down chairs and stepping over fallen chairs as they went.

Brock immediately ran toward one of the sets of double doors and started ushering people out, and he could see that Summer, Elle, and Everett were doing the same at the other doors. All fifty ambassadors had mobilized, helping people make their way out of the jumble of chairs and get outside. Most of the prospective students were holding over their heads the drawstring backpacks they'd given them at check-in that were filled with their packets. Some parents used jackets or cardigans as shelter, and many just ducked and ran.

Once they'd gotten the last of the Aquamoose Tracks participants out of the ballroom, they headed out, too. And then he heaved a sigh of relief that the sprinklers had gone off only in the ballroom and not the entire building. When they got down the stairs and outside, they could see that

Campus Security had led everyone to the grass on the quad.

People were shaking the water off their backpacks, brushing it off their arms, shaking out their hair. A loud, hyperactive chatter hung over the crowd. He took off his glasses and tried to find a spot on his shirt that was dry enough to wipe the water from his lenses.

Summer matched his stride as she ran her fingers through her hair, shaking out at least some of the water. "You had a dream that there was a flood during our presentations, right? Any other nightmares I need to be aware of?"

He shook his head and laughed. "I guess we're in luck, because other than the one about forgetting the schedule, my only nightmare was that I wore my clothes inside out."

"Whew. Okay, I'm going to go get us organized." One of the Campus Security officers handed her a megaphone and she strode to the front of the crowd.

Brock watched in amazement as Summer got everyone's attention and got them seated on the grass, sending a few ambassadors away to get chairs for the ones who needed them. Then she finished her presentation without the use of her slides or video and somehow managed to keep them engaged and laughing. She kept her cool so well and pivoted to do something different so seamlessly, even when everything (or at least water) came crashing down on them.

He looked around at the soaked crowd. Okay, maybe it *was*, in fact, impossible to plan for every outcome.

"And we are now ready for the campus tours!" Summer said through the megaphone. "We'll get you into groups with your assigned ambassadors and they'll lead you on the tour. Right after that, you and anyone you brought with you will go with your assigned ambassadors to dinner at Aquamoose Eats, LBSU's dining hall. That's upstairs in the Student Center, right between the giant living room area and the now-flooded ballroom.

"Then you'll say goodbye to your parents or guardians and meet right back here at six-fifteen. It's a warm enough afternoon so, hopefully, you'll be all the way dry by then. Thank you, everyone, parents and guardians especially, for being such good sports through all of this.

"Okay, look on the back of the name tag you've got on your lanyard—there should be a number between one and twenty-five. Since we're no longer in the ballroom where there were numbers on the wall for you to find your group, we're going to do this a little differently.

"Ambassadors one through ten—line up in order all along this side. Hold up your fingers high to show what number you are. Ambassadors eleven through twenty, you're on this side. Twenty-one through twenty-five, you're at the back. Alright, go find your group!"

As each of the groups headed in different directions to

see the campus, Brock, Summer, Everett, and Elle all made their way to each other.

"Well," Elle said, "this is definitely going to be one of the more memorable Aquamoose Tracks events we've held."

"Did anyone get pictures?" Everett asked. "Because I feel like this should be documented. No? I might have to email the students and have them send in their pics. Maybe make a contest with prizes."

Brock chuckled, and then met Summer's eyes. "I am impressed at how well you pulled everyone together after all that."

Instead of brushing off the compliment, she kept her eyes on him and gave him a very earnest, "Thank you." Then she said, "And I'm impressed at how well you made your presentation of a potentially boring topic not be boring. It was rather riveting. I think this contest will end with us closer in points than I'd guessed it would."

He smiled and chuckled. "Thank you."

"No, really. I didn't think that was possible, but you proved me wrong." And then she gave him a look that made him feel like he kind of already won.

Chapter Eleven

SUMMER

As the prospective students picked up all the paper airplanes from the quad and sailed them into the garbage cans, Brock, Elle, and Everett joined Summer at the top of the quad.

"Congratulations, you two," Everett said to Summer and Brock. "You've managed to smooth things over with the parents who weren't so happy about the unplanned sprinklers, you got three hundred thirty-seven people toured and fed, you've got the parents off, the paper airplane contest was a success, Baldy the Aquamoose crowned the winners, and you did it all without another single big disaster."

"I say that deserves a high five," Summer said, and all four of them went in for an awkward group high five.

"I better go do my thing," Brock said, and grabbed the megaphone, calling for everyone to gather in.

"You are all in luck, because Aquamoose Tracks is always on a Friday night and there is only one Friday night football game during the entire football season, and we always make sure that Aquamoose Tracks falls on the same night as it. So this is the only session you can attend all year where you'll experience the thrill of an Aquamoose football game.

"We are going to head over to the stadium now. You'll be going with the same two ambassadors you went on the campus tour and to dinner with; they've got your tickets. One of the two of them, along with the other roommates in their suite, will be your hosts for the night. They'll let you know which dorm you'll be heading back to right after the game. Now, who's ready to experience a Lake Baldwin State football game?"

He waited for the cheering to die down just a bit, and Summer just smiled up at him. He was just so cute up there. This may not have been the role he would've chosen to play if Tess had given him a choice in the matter—she knew he didn't prefer to be in front of a crowd—but he'd been a good sport and was actually surprisingly good at it. The students seemed to really love him. He had been growing on her a bit, too.

Okay, maybe a *lot*.

"If you're from around here," Brock called out, "you'll

know that we love our Aquamoose football. We get so much support from not only the residents of Lake Baldwin but also the two towns closest to us, Golden Springs and Sunrise. And many people further out than that.

"The population of Lake Baldwin City is about six thousand during the summers. About six thousand students go to Lake Baldwin State University, so the population of the city nearly doubles during the school year. But on game days, the population *of the football stadium alone* is fourteen thousand."

Summer smiled right along with Everett and Elle as they listened to the crowd's boisterous reactions. "Another thing we love here is our school's signature Aquamoose Tracks ice cream with the sweet ribbons of teal and purple running through it. Make sure you grab one from those coolers on your way. Now, let's go join them!"

As all the ambassadors headed across campus toward the stadium, and Brock headed toward Summer, Everett said, "Okay, and we're out."

"You're not staying for the game?" Summer asked Everett and Elle.

"I'm not," Elle said. "I've got a date."

"Someone new?" Summer asked.

Elle just nodded and smiled and Summer could tell she was looking forward to this one.

"I'm meeting friends to watch," Everett said. "Unless you need me to cover for you."

Summer shook her head. "Nope. Brock and I have got it. You go have fun."

The afternoon had been both exhausting and energizing—for different reasons and kind of for the same reasons—so she and Brock took the walk to the stadium slow and easy. As they walked, they talked about the event, their favorite parts about going to school at LBSU, and a little about work.

"What's your biggest regret from when you were in college?" she asked.

"*The* biggest? I feel like coming up with that answer would involve a spreadsheet and a ranking system and a complete accounting of four years of my life."

She laughed and shook her head. She should've known better than to ask him a question that had only one possible answer. "Okay, let me ask this instead: what is a regret from your college days that first comes to mind?"

"Ahh, that's a lot easier. Let's see...Okay, my junior year, first semester, I had Gallagher for Marketing Principles. I poured so much work into every assignment and did every extra credit assignment he offered, because I'd heard that his tests were so difficult, and I wanted to give myself a cushion so I could still get an A.

"Then, on the last day of instruction, he told us that it was his last semester teaching, so he decided to do something different for the final. We had two choices—we could either take the final test, and it would account for one hundred percent of our grade. So whatever we got on that test was our grade and none of the work we had done all semester would matter. Which was great if you were failing the class and completely maddening if you had worked your hardest.

"Or we could take option two—skip the final altogether and take a one-step drop in our grade. And no, going from a one hundred point three percent, which is essentially an A-plus, would *not* take our grade down to an A. I asked. It was right before Christmas and that was the semester that I took Financial Institutions and Markets."

"That class that you told the student on the tour had a homework load that could kill you?"

"That's the one. I didn't have enough time to study the amount it would take to ace the test, so I took the A-minus."

Summer gasped the amount that seemed appropriate, knowing what she knew of Brock.

"That one class ruined my four-point-oh GPA. I've regretted making the choice to just not put in the effort to ace that test ever since."

"Please tell me you rated him poorly for fairness on *Rate My Professor*, even though it was his last semester."

Brock chuckled. "I most definitely did. It helped. Okay, your turn. What's the college regret that first comes to mind for you?"

She didn't like thinking of regrets. Why did she ask him a question that she didn't know the answer to when she knew he'd ask her the same question? "I don't know. I guess just not sticking with a degree long enough to really master it. Although I'm not entirely sure I would be willing to give up any of the knowledge I gained from choosing a variety of majors."

He nodded like he understood, and she thought that he maybe did kind of understand.

It felt so...normal and comfortable talking about anything and everything and walking next to him. Yet, at the same time, it felt new and exciting and full of adventure.

She had always thought that the Brock she'd known from work—the rule follower, the guy who could see exactly how things should be and exactly what was wrong, the guy who expected a little too much perfection out of everyone and himself, including a perfect 4.0 GPA—was the way he was all of his waking hours.

But she'd seen such a different side of him today— actually, not just today, but through a lot of their planning over the past three weeks—that made her realize that he wasn't only about rules and perfection. He also knew how to have fun. To put perfection aside and connect with a crowd.

To connect with prospective students.

To connect with her.

Maybe what she had been interpreting as striving for perfection through the years they'd worked together had actually been the way his strong passion for what he was doing shone through. And she realized that her passion wasn't all that different from his.

As they angled their walking to the right at a fork in the sidewalk, they were closer together for a small moment, the knuckles of their hands brushing. It was the slightest touch, yet it sent thrills of peaceful joy through her.

Connecting with people was her thing. It ruled her waking hours. She connected with her best friend, her colleagues, her dad, people who worked at the stores where she shopped, the mailman, students, guys she went on dates with, everyone who worked at LBSU, everyone who showed up at the tri-town meet-up at Lake Baldwin, random people she passed on the street. She purposefully connected with people constantly. So how was it that her connection with Brock felt so much deeper than any of the others?

And how long had they had that connection? Had it been building the entire four years that she'd known him and she just hadn't realized how deep it had become? Or had it been shallow until Tess assigned them to work on Aquamoose Tracks together? She wasn't sure anymore.

By the time they got to the game, the ambassadors and prospective students had long since made it inside and found their seats. Summer and Brock took the seats she always sat in on the top row of the home side, where her ambassadors knew where to find her if they needed her. She could keep an eye on things, yet still let the ambassadors do their thing without interference so the prospective students could get more of a feel of college life.

The rowdy crowd of the full stadium quieted for a moment as the national anthem was sung and the ball was kicked off. Then the crowd cycled between cheering and anticipation, groaning and excitement, worry and happiness, foam fingers bouncing, teal and purple growl towels waving, moose-antler capped heads constantly in motion.

And Summer and Brock joined in with the crowd, too, cheering on the team that had been theirs since each of them first got their acceptance letters during their senior years in high school.

Then, as the first quarter neared its end, the sun began to set on the horizon, throwing brilliant purples and pinks and oranges and golds across the sky and the wisps of clouds, and suddenly it no longer mattered what was going on around them.

Brock reached out his hand, hesitant for the smallest moment before he entwined his fingers in hers. She responded by snuggling in close to him, resting her head against his shoulder.

It no longer mattered that they were surrounded by fourteen thousand enthusiastic fans watching a hometown football team at the beginning of a promising season who were really rocking it on the field. They were in a world by themselves, at the start of something new and beautiful, and she couldn't imagine being more blissful.

Remarkably, not a single ambassador came to her with an issue during the game. Possibly because it had been such an action-packed nail-biter of a game, so no one had time to worry about anything else.

Once it was over and everyone started exiting the stands, hoarse from so much cheering and exhausted from all the adrenaline, she and Brock joined the Aquamoose Tracks group to say goodbye and remind them to go straight to the dorms and that they would see them at nine in the morning for breakfast.

"This was a great game for them to experience," Brock said as they collapsed onto a bench, one of the few remaining people in the stands. "That's got to get them excited about going here."

Summer nodded. "We couldn't have planned that better." And then she chuckled, just thinking about how their planning had gone during their presentations. "Are you as exhausted as I am?"

"Definitely."

But he was sitting right next to her, and suddenly all of her nerve endings weren't so tired anymore. Brock reached out and ran a couple of fingers from the side of her forehead, down the edge of her hairline, brushing her hair out of her face—hair that was probably looking mighty crazy from the rain in the ballroom. "You're beautiful," he whispered, and it sounded like the most authentic thing she had ever heard. As if even in her exhausted, recently-drenched state, he still honestly found her beautiful.

There was something about him seeing her in a very un-perfect state and seeming to see her as perfect that made her heart melt.

"You're not so bad yourself," she said as she smiled at the hair on the top of his head that was always perfectly tousled, like it was the one rebellion he allowed himself, but was currently ever so slightly curly from how it dried after being soaked.

And then she looked into those dark eyes with the dark lashes and dark eyebrows and dark glasses frames and saw a light that she was so drawn to. A light that shone through everything that showed how much he cared about people. He ran a hand down the sleeve of her light jacket, and it sent shivers all up her spine.

Then she grabbed his face with both hands, like she couldn't stand to wait another moment, and kissed him. He slid his arm around her waist, pulling her a little closer as his lips moved against hers, cautious and careful, gentle and sweet. Like she was precious to him. She lost herself in the kiss, letting herself feel what it was like to kiss this man that she'd known for so long, seeming to feel every emotion he was pouring into the kiss, too.

After a moment, she pulled back from the kiss, touching her forehead against his. "I guess I shouldn't be surprised, since you are you, but that kiss was perfect."

She felt the rumble of his soft chuckle as much as she heard it. "That's almost exactly the same words I was thinking about you."

Chapter Twelve

BROCK

It always amazed Brock how quickly one hundred fifty high school seniors and fifty college students could completely devour every last breakfast item filling four long banquet tables on the grass in the quad.

He turned to Everett. "Did we eat that much when we were their age?"

Everett popped the last bite of his blueberry muffin in his mouth and then patted his stomach. "Some of us still do."

Once every scrap of food was gone, it wasn't too hard to get the reenergized students in the same groups they had been in yesterday.

Summer turned on the megaphone and held it to her mouth. "Raise your hand if at least one person in your group has installed the app for the scavenger hunt on your phone."

As two hundred hands went in the air, Brock couldn't help but smile at even the sound of Summer's voice. How had he heard that voice for so many years and hadn't realized how joyful it sounded?

She must've felt his eyes on her because she met his and gave him a smile and a wink that made his heart skip a beat from the backflip it just did.

"Future Aquamoose, do you understand your assignment?"

"Yes, ma'am!" a few of them called out.

"And you're ready to go?"

"Yes, ma'am!" Most of them said it in unison this time, which was rather impressive in its unplanned-ness.

"Ambassadors, are you ready?" They all gave her the thumbs up. "You've got exactly forty-five minutes to get pictures of all the items on campus that are listed in the app and arrive back here. And..." she said, dragging out the word, "go!"

As all of them scattered by groups in all different directions, Brock and Summer started setting up one obstacle course, and Elle and Everett got to work setting up the other one. They had already spray painted the grass to mark where each obstacle went and all the pool noodles that needed to be tied together were already tied, so the setup should go quickly. It was just a matter of getting everything in place on the quad.

As they were hammering in the garden stakes that would hold some pool noodles vertically that the players would have to weave between, and some that would make arches they would have to crawl under, Brock kept thinking about Summer kissing him last night and how amazing it had been. The entire football game had been pretty memorable. In fact, every bit of yesterday had been pretty unforgettable, rain in the ballroom and all.

As they were working together to tie two ropes from a hula hoop to a tree branch that stretched out nearly parallel to the ground, standing so close together, their hands working in the same space, Summer reached out a pinky and linked it in his and then gave him a smile that melted his insides.

He cleared his throat and said what he'd been thinking, even though he hadn't meant to. Actually, it was just a part of what he'd been thinking, since the other part had been imagining kissing her again. "So, how are you feeling about that kiss last night?"

"Like I've spent my whole life not being properly kissed, and now that I've experienced it, I'm a bit hooked. Can a person get addicted after just one kiss?"

He chuckled. "I also kissed you at your car last night, so it was two kisses."

"I was addicted after the first, though."

"What I wouldn't give to make it number three right now."

She bit her bottom lip, and he could tell that she was imagining the same thing. "Okay, setting up this obstacle course isn't enough of a distraction from thoughts of that. Tell me something."

"Like what?"

She waved her hand around. "I don't know. Um...Oh! Tell me about a great day you had as a kid. One where you went to bed just thinking everything had turned out awesome."

He pulled his head back. "Let me think. Okay, I was in ninth grade, and I had a day where I was perfect. I got a perfect score on a biology test that I had been so stressed about. I played basketball with friends for a few minutes and—I'm not even exaggerating—made every single shot. I had a list of 'dailies' that I tried to do every day, and I did every single one of them. I wasn't late to school or any of my classes, I got all my chores and my homework done by the time I was supposed to finish, and I was in bed by ten. I just lay there before falling asleep, thinking about how every single thing had gone perfectly, and wondering if I could duplicate that success every day."

Summer chuckled. "Oh, I totally should've guessed something like that was your great day. And do you know what? Thinking about fourteen or fifteen-year-old you being so thrilled about a day like that kind of makes me want to kiss you more."

He winked. "I guess your distraction plan is foiled." As they moved on to tying the jump ropes (that he had gone back to Taheny's to buy) between garden stakes, making an obstacle they'd have to step over, he said, "Maybe telling me a great day you had as a kid will help."

She looked at him for a long moment, her eyes flicking to his lips a few times. "Okay, I'm willing to give it a shot. I was turning eight, and my mom was in Fiji or somewhere, and my dad was super busy with work, and I knew no one was going to plan my birthday party, so I planned it myself. I didn't just invite my entire class—I invited my entire grade."

Brock laughed. "Please tell me you planned it for a time when your dad would be home."

Summer grabbed another jumprope and started tying it to the next stake. "Nope. My parents hired out everything, though, so I planned it for a time when I knew the landscape company would have someone mowing the lawn, and when my nanny would be home taking care of me. I figured the parents of the kids I invited would assume they were my parents and be comfortable dropping their kids off. And they did."

"Did your nanny know about it ahead of time?"

"I kept everything a total secret. Nobody saw all my preparations for the games, my dad didn't notice that I borrowed his credit card to order cupcakes online from a local bakery that delivered, and no one saw the invitations that I'd spent days making. It was a surprise to everyone when a total of forty-eight kids showed up at my house. And let me tell you, it was a smashing success. It was all kids talked about at school for weeks."

"And your dad never knew?"

"Oh, he knew. He canceled a meeting so he could come home early on my birthday to surprise me, and then he got the bigger surprise. I think there was a part of him that was impressed that I pulled off such a great party on my own. I went to bed that night with a giant smile on my face. Not only had I impressed my dad, but I had impressed myself. It kind of gave me the knowledge that I could accomplish anything I needed to on my own. I felt strong and independent and confident."

He looked at her for a long moment, simultaneously being impressed and sad that she'd had to get that realization at such a young age, and then said, "Okay, well that story makes me want to kiss you, so we are completely failing at this."

"At least we are winning at this," she said, motioning to their course. Then she called out loud enough for Elle and Everett to hear, "Hey, slowpokes. How's it coming along over there?"

"Just a few troubles," Elle said, grunting each word as

they tried to force their unruly pool noodles into a big arch. "Nothing we can't handle."

The four of them barely got both obstacle courses finished before the first of the teams came back from the scavenger hunts, and then all four of them were busy checking off the winners' findings and, once everyone had returned, awarding the winners with LBSU swag.

Then Summer and Brock showed the obstacle courses to the students and explained that each group of six needed to choose one person from their team to go through the course blindfolded. Everyone else on the team could shout out instructions, but they couldn't touch the person going through the course. And then they started the contests, timing each person as they went, Brock and Summer manning one course and Elle and Everett on the other.

They were on opposite sides of the course—Summer on one side, tying the blindfold on the person competing, and Brock at the other end, timing each competitor. Yet they still caught each other's eye a lot of times, and it made Brock's heart leap, just like the student jumping over the jumprope obstacles. There were plenty of times when they were closer, too, and just happened to brush hands or shoulders. A little subtle touch that sent thrills through him.

Once each team had a chance to compete, they were about to award swag to the teams with the top times, but then someone called out, "Wait! We want Summer and Brock to go through it!"

And then the entire group started chanting "Summer and Brock." Even the ambassadors were joining in.

He looked at Summer. "Do you want to do this?"

She nodded. "I'm all in." And he suddenly wondered if she was talking about the course.

Elle tied the blindfold on Summer, and then took her hand to lead her to the starting line. Then Everett, who had been holding a timer, said, "Go!"

Brock stood right next to her, just far enough away that they weren't touching, and said, "Okay, we're at the jump ropes. Move forward the length of your foot. Okay, now step up. A little higher. Okay, you're over. Take a big step. A little shuffle. Okay, you're at the next one."

On and on, under the arches, between the vertical pool noodles, in and out and in and out of the water jug mines, stepping into the middle of each of the pool noodle rings, and across the wooden plank, he kept his voice calm and quiet amid the chaos of the cheering students, letting her know that he wouldn't lead her astray.

"You're at the last obstacle—the hula hoop. Reach your hands out, yeah, right there."

"Make it in ten seconds and you have the top time!" Everett called out.

"Okay, lift one leg. A little higher. Okay, now put it through the hoop."

The crowd was counting down now as one. "Five, four…"

"Okay, you've almost got that foot to the ground. Got it. Okay, now—"

He could tell the moment she stopped listening to him and listened to the crowd stressing the time because she sped up, catching her foot on the bottom of the hula hoop, causing her to face plant in the grass instead of finishing with what he was sure would've been a graceful motion.

The moment she hit the ground, she started laughing and couldn't seem to stop, which made him start laughing, too. She reached up and pulled the blindfold off her eyes and grinned up at him as he offered her a hand up. She took it and pulled herself up, then bowed to the crowd. "Okay, winners, I think your record time is safe. Let's get them some swag!"

They finished up the event, giving the prospective students final words and instructions on how to they could waive the application fee since they came to Aquamoose Tracks, reminded them to take home everything they'd brought, told them to email if they had any questions, then told them that they couldn't wait to see them next fall.

Once all the students had dispersed, the ambassadors helped them to clean everything up and haul it back to the staging room in the Welcome Center before heading back to their dorms.

Exhausted, Brock walked Summer to her car. "So do

you typically go home after Aquamoose Tracks and crash for the rest of the day?"

Summer laughed. "Yes, but only for an hour, because there's just too much to fit into a Saturday to sleep long. Later, I'll go with Valeria to the tri-town meet-up at Lake Baldwin, like I do every Saturday night. And this time Avery is going with us."

That sounded so tiring after all they'd done in the previous day and a half. He leaned against Summer's car and nudged his glasses up, trying not to stare at how beautiful Summer was. Then he decided he didn't want to keep from staring and just took her in.

A smile tugged at her lips, and she looked down for a moment, possibly embarrassed. But then she looked back up and met his eyes, so he took the moment to ask a question he'd been dying to ask. "Do you want to go on a real date with me?"

"A real date?"

"You know, something traditionally date-ish. Like going to a movie or dinner or bowling."

"If we go bowling, can we eat bowling alley food?"

Brock tipped his head to the side. "Bowling alley food?"

"Yeah. You know—low-quality burgers, fantastic fries with ranch, soda."

He smiled. "Then yes, we can."

Summer stepped closer to him, her foot bumping

against his, their legs almost touching. "Okay, but I feel like I need to warn you that I was in a bowling league for three weeks when I was younger."

His eyebrow rose.

"So be prepared to play with a pro. Oh, and I have the perfect bowling outfit. I can't wait for you to see it."

He couldn't help the smile that spread across his face. "I can't wait, either. Does next Friday work?"

She nodded. "Friday it is. Now can I have that kiss that I've been dying to get all morning?"

He was still smiling when his lips first touched hers.

Chapter Thirteen

SUMMER

Summer, Valeria, and Avery all stepped out of her car and walked to the shore of Lake Baldwin for the tri-town meet-up.

"Oh my heck specks, that's a lot of people," Avery breathed.

Summer grinned. "I know. Isn't it great? Let me show you around."

As they walked to the heart of the action, Summer and Valeria both said hi to people, gave out lots of hugs, asked about people's dogs and jobs and significant others and whatever else had seemed important to them the last time they'd chatted, and she introduced Avery to all of them.

Then, when they'd gotten to the middle of everything, still far enough away from the water that they were at the top of the slope and could see everything, Summer started pointing it all out to Avery. As usual, someone was playing music from big speakers, which always kind of worked as the soundtrack for everything going on.

"There are always people showing off dance moves right there in front of the speakers. And games—always beach volleyball, but people bring different beach games every time. Those are fun. And people playing hacky sack or throwing a football. And lots of food trucks. Are you hungry? We've got a bit of everything. There are lots of tables to eat at or play cards or just hang out. Anyway, lots of people to talk to, meet, mingle with, get to know. Oh, look! There's Deja down on the shore dancing with her man."

Avery seemed a bit overwhelmed, so they stayed together for the first while and chatted with a bunch of groups of people until Avery got really invested in a conversation with a cute guy.

Summer felt her phone buzz, so she pulled it out and saw a text from her dad saying hi and asking her what kind of fun she was up to on a Saturday night. So she typed a quick text back saying hi and asking what he was up to, then snapped a quick picture of her with the group of people she was chatting with, the beach and all the people in the background, then sent it to him.

When they all met up again, Avery seemed much more excited about being there and a whole lot more comfortable in her surroundings, which was exactly what

Summer had been hoping for when she'd invited her to join them.

Summer glanced down at her watch. "Hey, do you two mind if I leave a bit early? I want to see if Brock is free."

Valeria shook her head. "No leaving early. It's only been something like ten hours since you saw him at Aquamoose Tracks."

"Okay..." Summer said, pulling out her phone. "What about if I call him to see if he wants to join us here, then?"

Valeria took her phone out of her hands and shoved it into Summer's back pocket. "Nope, not doing that either."

It was all so unlike Valeria, so she just looked at her in confusion. "Why?"

Valeria tapped a finger on her lip. "Let me try to think of an analogy for you." She looked out at the campfires on the beach. "Pouring gas on a fire? No...Oh! I know—I'll use your life."

"You want to use my life as an analogy for my love life?"

"Yes. Let's talk about your hobbies and how quickly you master them and move on. What was the last thing you decided you were going to pick up and learn?"

"Archery."

"And how long did that take?"

Summer shrugged. "A few weeks."

"And before that?"

"Cooking Thai food. A few weeks on that, too."

"And before that?"

"Hip hop dancing. That was hard—more than a month."

"And before that, guitar, up-cycling, photography, rock climbing..."

Summer nodded, not getting where Valeria was going with this at all.

"You pour all of your focus into a new hobby, and then you're done. You move on to a new one."

"Well, yeah, because it's about the challenge. So once I master something, what's the point of continuing to do it? There are other interesting things out there."

Valeria nodded. "Which was pretty much your same philosophy in choosing a major."

Avery looked like she was trying to hold in a laugh, but a bit of it burst out. So she sipped her soda and gazed off at a crowd, acting like nothing had happened. Summer still didn't get where Valeria was going with any of this.

"Someone might assume that with your personality type and your ridiculous ability to master things quickly, you might move on from one job to another quickly, too. You'd master one, then move to another. And every few years, you'd move on to a new career altogether. Yet you've stayed at the Welcome Center since you were eighteen. *Nine years.* For someone with your personality type, that's like...a lifetime."

"Well, yeah. It's my home."

"Avery," Valeria said, "help me out here. How long have you worked with Summer?"

"I started just over three years ago in admissions, about a month before Summer started full time in the Welcome Center."

"And have you noticed anything different between Brock and Summer over the past few weeks?"

"Yeah," Avery dreamily said. "They smile differently."

Summer looked over at her coworker. "*What?*"

"Well, you definitely smile differently when you're around each other, of course. But it's not only that. It's like even when you're not thinking of each other, there's still a part of you that is, and it changes your smile."

Summer smiled, just thinking of Brock smiling differently when he thought of her.

"Huh," Valeria said, studying Avery. "Observant girl. Have you seen either of them be like that before?"

"Not really. Never with Brock. I've seen it on Summer a few times before, but it never lasted more than a day. And never like this."

Wow. She hadn't even realized that about herself, let alone about Brock. "Okay. I'm still not getting why me wanting to go hang out with Brock instead of hanging out with seventy-five of my favorite people is problematic."

Valeria met her eyes. "Are you ready for things to get serious with Brock?"

"That's not something I usually ask myself when I'm in 'about to go on a first date' territory."

"Do you ever ask yourself if you're ready for things to get serious with anyone?"

She crossed her arm and looked at her roommate. "So I don't usually think about getting serious. That's not a big deal." It probably was a big deal and she knew it; she just really didn't like to think about it. She didn't even know what about it made her skirt the topic so much.

"With Brock," Valeria said, "maybe you should spend some time thinking about it. Because dating him comes with more consequences than the men you normally date."

"We've been friends and coworkers for a long time. If we started a relationship and it ended, we could just go back to being friends and coworkers." She might not have always believed that, but now that she really *wanted* to date him, it didn't seem like it was much of an issue.

Valeria was giving her a look like her comment was so absurd that she had no words. So Avery stepped in. "I don't think that's really how relationships work. They kind of only go forward or they end."

Valeria nodded. "Like I said, *consequences*. And I'm talking consequences beyond things just feeling awkward at work."

Avery nodded. "You stick with the Welcome Center because it's home. Maybe Brock is your home, too."

"Exactly, *chica.*" Valeria poked her in the shoulder with her pointer finger to drive the point home. "So make sure you're not treating your relationship with him like you do a hobby. And when things do start to get more serious, maybe rethink your inclination to run."

————

WHEN SUMMER first stepped foot into the Student Center on Monday morning, she could hear the industrial fans still blowing on the carpet in the ballroom upstairs.

And the first thing she noticed when she walked into the lobby of the Welcome Center was Pavani. She ran up to her friend and coworker and gave her a long hug. "Does this mean you're back?"

Pavani grinned. "I am. Well, my doctor only approved me for half time this week, but I should be back to full time next week! How was Aquamoose Tracks? Did the sprinklers really come on in the ballroom?"

"Right in the middle of my presentation. But it went well. I've got to go meet with the ambassadors who are working today, but I think we're going over the feedback forms first thing, so you'll get to hear from the horse's mouth how it went."

It was all Summer could do to make herself go to the right and down the hall to the big meeting room to meet with the five students working today instead of going left through the doorway into their office area to see Brock. But somehow she managed it and ran the morning meeting with Alejandro, Paige, Jessa, Takeshi, and McKay and gave them their assignments for the day, and only cut it short by a few minutes.

Then she went into the office area and her eyes met Brock's through the glass as he sat at his desk, talking on the phone. Seeing his face didn't just make her face smile, it made her entire soul smile. He gave her a pretty glorious smile back. She had gone nearly two full days—forty-five hours—without seeing Brock, which had given her a good amount of time to think about what she really wanted. And to really miss him. Following Valeria's advice had nearly killed her.

She set her things down in her office, and when she stepped back out, Brock was just coming out of his office. Then Tess walked down the hall leading from her office and said, "Summer, Brock, will you come to my office for a moment before the morning meeting?"

They followed Tess down the hallway, and Summer glanced at Brock, giving him a questioning look, but he just shrugged. When they reached the doorway of Tess's office, he touched Summer's lower back ever so slightly, a cue to say she could go in first, and she drank in the slight contact.

Once they were all seated, Tess picked up a stack of papers from her desk, tapping them on the desk to straighten them. "I was looking through all the feedback forms from Aquamoose Tracks, and I started noticing a trend in the 'Anything you would like to tell us about the event?' section. I'd like to read a couple of them to give you an idea."

She set the stack down again and picked up the top paper. "'Summer and Brock make the cutest couple! Did they meet at LBSU? I want to hear their story.' And another. 'Summer and Brock were so adorable together! I hope that by the time I go to school here, they're married!'" She put the papers down and looked at both of them. "Are you two an item now?"

The sensation of Summer's face suddenly being sunburned was returning in full force. In front of her boss wasn't exactly where she wanted to have this conversation with Brock. Or to hear what the prospective students thought of it.

"Um…" She looked at Brock, and he looked at her, seeming to not quite know what to say any more than she did. "Everything is still so new—we haven't exactly had a chance to discuss stuff like that."

At the same time, Brock said, "Yeah, I think we are."

"We are?"

"I mean I want to be an item with you. To date you."

She smiled. "I do, too."

Tess leaned back in her chair. "This is a far cry from

when you both were in here three weeks ago and I told you that you'd be working together."

They both chuckled, and Brock rubbed the back of his neck. "Yeah, I know."

"I don't know whether to congratulate you both on getting past your differences or be worried for you."

Summer sat up straighter. "Worried?"

"Well," Tess said, motioning at Summer, "you take a chance on everything, whether you think it'll work out or not." Then she motioned at Brock. "And you don't take a chance on anything that isn't practically guaranteed to work out."

If Tess was right, then that meant Brock thought their relationship was "practically guaranteed to work out." She swallowed hard. "Does that mean you think I'm going to mess this up?"

Tess's voice softened. "No, Summer. Not at all. I'm just saying to proceed carefully. There aren't any rules against dating in this department. Don't make there be a reason for a new rule."

Summer nodded.

"Are you okay with everyone in the meeting seeing the evaluations that mention the two of you, or would you rather I pulled them first?"

Summer looked at Brock, but he shrugged then said, "I think it's fine to leave them in. I mean, Elle and Everett were there, so if the students picked up on it, they probably did, too. Summer?"

"I think it's fine. I already texted Pavani about it and Deja is smart enough and observant enough that she probably figured it out the second one of us walked in this morning. Or maybe she even knew before we did."

When they left Tess's office, Tess stayed inside, so Summer stopped Brock in the hall and whispered, "Do you think we're making a mistake?" She hadn't exactly had a lot of experience with relationships that had the potential to become serious, and Tess's hesitation about it was making Summer worry.

Brock ran a hand down her arm and then gave her hand a squeeze. "I think that dating you is the most correct decision I could ever make."

She exhaled every bit of her air in one smiling sigh.

As they headed out to the main area, Avery just happened to glance their direction from the other side of the half wall and gave her a grin and a wave. Summer waved back.

Evaluation meetings always took a while, so everyone got their water bottles and sat around the big table. Summer loved these meetings—they kind of felt like a big family dinner. There was also the excitement of talking about an event for over three hundred people that she had worked so hard on and had recently pulled off. She'd also had all fifty of the ambassadors together. The event always gave her such a high that stayed with her days.

And at this meeting, they got to hear all the things that students liked about it and all the things that they thought could make it better. It was thrilling.

Tess divided up all the feedback forms between the seven of them as she opened the meeting, and Summer started flipping through her twenty. They always read through the handwritten part at the bottom and shared with the group any positive feedback and any suggestions for improvement, and Deja kept track of all of it because the woman had superpowers and could somehow do the same thing everyone else was doing *and* take notes on it all.

Then they would each tally up the ratings the students had given for each of the individual parts and then combine them to find out the score for each of them.

Everett chuckled. "You've all got to hear this one. 'Props to Brock. If I worked with Summer, I'd want to date her, too.'" Everyone chuckled, too, but then Everett paused a moment and said, "Wait. Are you two dating?"

Summer just shook her head. Apparently, it wasn't obvious to *everyone*.

"Oh, I've got one, too," Elle said. "'I just wanted to give the heart-eyes emoji every time I saw Brock and Summer look at each other.' Aww. That's sweet."

Brock was sitting at Summer's right, and she almost

became a heart-eyes emoji herself when he reached under the table, away from everyone's view, to hold her hand.

Deja held a paper up. "I've got an 'I'm rooting for Summer and Brock. I hope those two crazy kids make it.' and then a hand-drawn emoji of..." She turned the paper to one side and then the other. "I think it's like that face with one eye bigger than another, an open mouth with the tongue hanging out. Or maybe it's a picture of a bowl of soup—hard to tell. High school students can be strange sometimes. Okay, I think at this point, we need to make a drinking game out of finding ones that mention Brock and Summer as a couple."

They got a lot of really good feedback from the forms. A lot of comments about the sprinklers, too. Elle held up a paper to read it out loud. "This one says 'I gave one star to the presentation about school activities because no one told me to dress in a raincoat and getting drenched wasn't cool at all.'"

"Toss out her rating on Summer's presentation," Tess said, "since it wasn't based on the presentation."

Whew. She didn't want that score against her.

"I've got one, too," Pavani said. "'I gave five stars to Summer's presentation because choreographing an indoor rainstorm to happen during it was awesome. So was finishing it outside.'"

"Toss that one out, too," Tess said.

Bummer.

All during the meeting, Summer kept catching Tess looking at her, scrutinizing her. Like she was trying to decide if it was possible for things to work out between Summer and Brock. She obviously had a lot more reservations about Summer's ability than she did in Brock's ability. It made Summer wonder even more if she should be worried herself.

"I've got a Summer and Brock one!" Everett said, holding it up like he'd won a prize. "'Summer and Brock are about the cutest couple ever. Hashtag relationship goals.' Everyone drink!"

They all picked up their water bottles and took a drink.

Thirty minutes later, as they were getting close to finishing up all the evaluations, Deja said, "I think this is the most hydrated I've been all week. Thanks, Summer and Brock."

A few people chuckled, but Pavani just groaned. "If we keep drinking water at this pace, I'm going to have to leave the meeting early to pee."

Tess clapped once. "Okay, let's get the ratings tallied so we can all take a trip to the restrooms."

A few minutes after everyone wrote down the tallies of their twenty and slid them over to Deja, she said, "Okay, I've got the scores. I'll go through each of the different activities, but since I'm sure Brock and Summer both want to know who won, I'll start with those. Summer, you got a combined average of four point seven stars out of five."

"Wow!" Elle said. "That's so impressive, especially since you had to give half of your presentation outside without the visuals!"

Summer grinned. Four point seven was great. She had been perfecting the presentation for a while now, and she was happy with the changes she'd made for this year's events.

"And Brock got a whopping four point eight!"

"Whoa!" Everett said and then gave Brock a fist bump.

As everyone else congratulated Brock, Summer did, too, because whether she won or not, four point eight was well worthy of celebrating.

"I had one student sum both of them up perfectly," Pavani said, pulling a paper out of her stack. "'Summer's presentation made me want to go to LBSU, and Brock's made me feel like it was possible.'"

Huh. She hadn't guessed that they would pair up so well to help students decide to come to Lake Baldwin State. It was like they'd belonged together all along.

After the meeting, Summer had to head to the staging room to make sure everything was accounted for. Brock came in less than a minute later, and she turned to see him.

"Congratulations on winning. That last comment had to have made you feel great."

"It really did."

She took a step closer to him. "You know what you did by winning, right? You guaranteed that you'll get to be a bigger part of every single Aquamoose Tracks we have, even with Pavani back in the game."

He took a step closer to her. "Maybe that was my plan all along—I was just plotting a way to spend more time with you."

She closed the gap between them and breathed, "That makes you one clever man, Brock McMillan."

And then he wrapped his arm around her waist and pulled her in for a kiss.

Chapter Fourteen

BROCK

*B*rock leaned against the end of the counter in the bowling alley where he could wait for Summer with an unobstructed view of the front door. He had planned to pick her up at her apartment, but she had texted fifteen minutes before he was going to leave that she had to run something to a friend in need on the other side of town, so she would just meet him at the bowling alley on the way back.

He hadn't been on a date in several months, so he had to think back quite a bit to try to remember if he was always this nervous before a date, but he didn't think he was. Everything about Summer was different; he should just expect it to be that way by now. He ran his fingers through the top of his hair, smoothed down the front of his t-shirt, straightened his jeans, and fixed the way they fell over his shoes. He had planned everything for this date down to the last detail, with all the things he knew Summer would love, so he really didn't have any reason to be nervous.

The doors opened and, like a big ray of sunshine, Summer walked in, wearing the big, billowy yellow ballgown he had so rashly told her not to buy because she wouldn't have any place to wear it.

He was simultaneously feeling speechless at how beautiful she was and finding it hilarious that she had chosen to wear it bowling, of all places. And thinking that he one hundred percent should've anticipated it. All the emotions together appeared on his face as a big, goofy grin, and he didn't even care.

He walked up to her, kissed her on the cheek, and said, "You look beautiful in that dress."

She gave him a smile that seemed to have some mystery behind it, too, then dipped into a little curtsy. "Do you like my hair?"

It was pulled up in some kind of fancy twist with curls and pins with sparkly gems and showed off her beautiful neck and shoulders. "I love it. It goes really well with the dress. I still can't believe you wore it here."

"I told you I had the perfect outfit," she said as she put her hand in his and started walking toward the check-in counter.

"You did indeed tell me that."

The guy behind the counter finished up with the people in front of Brock and Summer, then he turned his attention on them. He looked Summer up and down, then in a monotone voice that somehow still managed to sound sarcastic, he said, "Nice bowling outfit."

He didn't like that the guy was mocking Summer and was opening his mouth to say something, but Summer beat him to it. "Right? That's exactly what I was telling my date!"

The guy's bored expression slowly turned to a smile of amusement as he helped them. She probably just made the guy's night and gave him a story to tell his coworkers.

As they carried the bowling shoes the guy had plunked down on the counter for them over to the lane they'd been assigned, Brock joked, "I'm not sure those shoes go with that dress."

"It's okay because I'm going to find a bowling ball that *will* go with it. I'm all about the accessories."

He wasn't sure how she was going to be able to bowl in a dress that floofed out so wide. But then she stood up, bowling shoes on, and gathered the many layers of the dress together at her left side, just above her knee, and tied it into a big knot. Then she stood tall—not like a model about to show off the newest fashion on the runway, but with her fists on her hip like a superhero about to go off and save the day.

He took in her whole appearance. The dress was just off her shoulders and fitted down to the waist, and now, with the knot on the side, everything from the waist almost to her knees was very big. Her bare legs looked pretty incredible, leading down to her brown and maroon bowling shoes. It might have been the cutest thing he'd ever seen.

Then they went to choose their bowling balls. Summer had been looking for a ten pound ball, but couldn't find one that went with her dress, so they searched in the racks along the back of all the lanes. About three-fourths of the way down, she spotted one that made her really excited and ran to it. It was a bright yellow, a pale yellow, and a white marbled ball, and she picked it up, saying, "This is perfect."

Brock found one that fit his hand size and was a good weight, then picked the one with the same size and weight that sat next to it, simply because it matched his blue shirt better. Summer grinned at him as she hefted her ball back to their lane.

"How many pounds is that one?" he asked as she plunked it down in their ball return.

"Fifteen."

"Can your hand even fit in the finger holes?"

"I'm pretty sure no."

"Summer, we can get you another ball."

"This one is perfect."

And so it was. They entered the names into the screen hanging from the ceiling and started bowling. He couldn't get enough of watching Summer bowl in her now-short ball gown as she held her ball with both hands, swinging it back by her right hip, and then sending it sailing down the lane. Every time, it would look like it was going to go into the gutter on the right side, but then the spin on the ball would take it back toward the center just before it got to the pins.

There were times when he was ahead in score, but she was ahead more often, so it was clearly working for her. Halfway through their first game, he noticed some teenagers start bowling a few lanes down from them, and they were amazing. Both of them were throwing the ball the same way that Summer was, and he suddenly wondered if she had learned that technique in her three weeks in a bowling league as a kid.

He high fived her as she was coming back to their table after getting a strike.

"You know," he said, "if you'd have told me you were going to wear that dress, I would've worn something to coordinate."

Her eyebrows rose, intrigued. "Do you own anything yellow?"

"I have a gray t-shirt with a one-inch stitched logo right here that's yellow. And I have yellow socks."

"Then we clearly missed an excellent opportunity."

Brock shrugged. "Next time, then."

He loved the smile that spread across Summer's face. He really wanted to kiss it.

When they had finished both of their games—one where he won by two points and one where she won by thirty-seven—and they'd taken a selfie with the screen showing their scores in the background, they headed over to the counter to order food.

Once they were seated at a table in the corner, he asked a question he'd wondered about several times over the years but had been wondering more and more often lately, since her choice was greatly affecting his life and level of happiness. "You're from Minneapolis, right? What made you choose to go to a college in South Dakota? Why LBSU?"

She smiled, then looked thoughtful, like she was thinking of the full answer instead of just giving whatever was her usual answer. "Well, I wanted to go to a small college so I would feel like I knew everyone, instead of going to a big school where I'd feel lost among so many students. And I wanted to go somewhere with a campus that I loved and could totally see myself calling home, around people who felt like home. And it had to be somewhere fun." She smiled. "The lake was a plus."

She paused like she was trying to get into where her head had been nine years ago. "Plus, I kind of felt...

trapped at home. Not physically trapped. Maybe trapped isn't even the right word. I guess I felt kind of *stuck* in the emotions that were too present in my house, so I wanted to get away, preferably to another state, so I would have to stay over the summer to establish residency. But I do love to see my dad as often as possible, so I didn't want to be more than an hour's flight away."

The same woman who had taken their order behind the counter brought over their food and set it on their table, so they took a moment and got the right burger and drink in front of each of them, the basket of fries between them, each with their own condiment cup of ranch dressing.

"How about you?" Summer asked as she picked up a fry and dipped it in the ranch. "What brought you here?"

"My reason is...a whole lot less complicated than yours. LBSU is twenty minutes from where I grew up in Golden Springs and I wanted to stay close to home so I could still help out easily. It was a no-brainer—it just happened to work out well for me."

"So you chose here to be close to your family and I chose here to get away from my family." Summer shook her head, chuckling. "I guess that right there shows which of us is the better person."

Brock chuckled, too, then said, "Nah. I think it shows which of us is the stronger person." He hadn't ever headed out on his own like that, but he knew it had to have been exponentially more difficult than being twenty minutes away like he was.

They picked up their hamburgers and took a bite. They had been joking around and laughing so much while they'd been bowling that he hadn't had a moment to stop and even think about the plan he'd made for their date. But now that they were sitting down and eating, he was thinking about it and realizing how much his plan wasn't going to work with Summer wearing that dress.

He might as well deal with it head-on instead of letting his focus stay on how to fix the problem instead of on his conversation with Summer. So he pulled the schedule out of his pocket and unfolded the notepaper. "The rest of my plan for tonight isn't going to work out as planned."

Summer's eyes went wide as she looked at his schedule. "Oh, wow, that is a really detailed plan."

His need to plan everything was probably going to start to annoy a woman like Summer, especially over time. And he really didn't want that to happen. But he just did better when he had a list for everything.

But he also really did better when he planned *well*. He had worked hard to come up with the perfect plan based on what he knew of Summer, and he didn't get that right at all. Obviously.

He could almost feel her eyes going down each item

on the list which, now that he was reading through it again, thinking about how she was seeing it, he wished he hadn't been so specific with each item. Especially with the one that read, *Arrive at Summer's house at 6:58. Make sure I'm looking really good, then head to her door right at 7:00, flowers in hand.*

"You were going to bring me flowers?"

He shrugged. "I'll do that another time. I was mostly referring to the parts after dinner."

Summer got a look of mock surprise on her face. "What? You don't want to go to the top of Lookout Hill, lay down a blanket, string some lights from the antenna of your truck to a nearby tree, and have our own little two-person ball?" She laughed and put a hand on his arm, sending a zing of sensations up his arm. "I'm totally kidding."

She tapped a finger on the part of his list that read, *Take a walk along the path leading around Lake Baldwin, and if the sky is as clear as the forecast shows, stargaze on the beach.* "I have a bag with jeans and a t-shirt in my car so I could change precisely because I thought you might want to do something exactly like this."

He smiled at Summer. Maybe he should stop trying to predict what she was going to do in any situation.

He couldn't imagine he would ever give up his list-making or over-preparing—he liked those things about himself. But he had been trying hard to be less rigid and more spontaneous. Summer had brought that side of him out, and he was enjoying it. But it was something he had to push himself to do, and tonight, being spontaneous sounded amazing.

"Actually, your plan sounds even better. Let's do that."

"What? Why? I don't mind changing clothes."

"I once told you that you had nowhere to wear that dress, and I was very clearly wrong. I've since been trying to eat my words as gracefully as possible, but I think you deserve to have a ball to wear it to, even if it's a two-person ball."

Her smile lit up her whole face. Possibly the whole bowling alley.

"My truck has an outlet, but I don't—"

She grabbed his arm. "Your truck has an actual outlet?"

He nodded.

"I have a string of lights! Don't give me a look like it's weird to have a string of lights in my trunk—it's in the bin of supplies I take into high schools for my presentation. Plus, I like to be prepared. I also have a hammock, a football, a few hoodies, a swimsuit and a towel, and phone chargers for both iPhone and Samsung, because you never know where an adventure is going to take you. Not that we'll need all those things, but I do have a Bluetooth speaker, so we can have music at our ball."

"And I have a blanket."

"Perfect!" She stood up, and they grabbed all their trash and threw it away before heading out to her car to gather her supplies, and then they got in his truck.

A few minutes later, they came to the end of the dirt road that led around and around Lookout Hill—which could barely be called a hill—before ending at the top. With as flat as the entire eastern side of South Dakota was, on a clear day they could pretty much stand on a tuna can and see all the way to Saint Paul. So the little hill gave them a great view of the entire town.

He pulled within a dozen feet of the lone tree on the hill, and after a few minutes, they had the lights strung from his antenna to the tree, the blanket spread out under the lights, and the Bluetooth speaker playing soft music.

Summer untied the knot at the side of her dress and let the skirt fall in a beautiful wave toward the blanket-covered ground, and he'd never felt so underdressed for an occasion yet completely comfortable with the feeling.

He pretended that he was dressed in something much fancier than a t-shirt and jeans and gave her a slight bow, his arm bent in front of his waist. "May I have this dance?"

She gave him a curtsy and said, "I would love nothing more."

He put an arm around her waist and she put her arm around his neck, and they held hands and danced around their little bit of space on the blanket. He had never really known much about how to dance, but it still felt so nice to be moving as one with Summer in time to the music. Back when he'd been making plans for this date, he'd imagined how it would be to walk around the lake with Summer, hand-in-hand, and knew it would be amazing.

This was so much better, though. He was kind of liking this more spontaneous version of himself that she coaxed out.

After a while, she laid her head against his shoulder, and they swayed to the music as they looked out at all the lights in the town, shining in the darkness, and the way the moon reflected on the lake, not far off to their left. Crickets in the distance made their own music, adding to the music coming from the speakers, and he couldn't imagine a moment more perfect.

Without lifting her head from his shoulder, she asked, "Where do you think you'll be working in five years from now?"

He was surprised by the question. But maybe he shouldn't have been—being a recruiter was a tough job. All of the on-location recruiters they had usually burnt out within three to four years and went to the private sector, usually for sales jobs, so their department had a fair amount of turnover. But he wasn't a recruiter. "Right where I am, only with a lot more businesses on board with donating scholarships. In a place where I can get as many kids able to get a college education as possible. Or, if I can do that better in another position at Lake

Baldwin State, then I'll do that, but I'd like to stay where I am."

She lifted her head and looked at him for a long moment, and he couldn't quite interpret the look on her face. Eventually, he said, "What about you? What are your plans for the future?"

She took his hand and sat on the blanket, pulling him down to sit next to her. He put his arms behind him on the blanket to support them, and she snuggled into the space beside him. He took a moment to breathe in the scent of sunshine and citrus on her, to take in the feel of her next to him.

"Staying at LBSU, of course. But also having kids."

"Oh yeah?" He wanted kids, too, and was interested to hear more.

"Like ten of them."

"Ten?" The number hit him hard, like a physical blow.

"Well, some number around there—it doesn't have to be ten. I like people a lot. I think I would like my own little people a *whole* lot." She looked out at the lights in the town. "And I think I would make a great mom. I mean, I didn't exactly have the best mom as an example, but I have my dad, and I had a lot of friends with amazing moms. I want to give my kids all the love and attention and nurturing that I didn't get. You know, bring the Graham Family Mothering Average up to more stellar levels."

He studied her for a moment. "How did you grow up

with the kind of upbringing that you did and not turn out to be a bitter, people-hating person?"

"I need people." She shrugged. "Well, I mean, every single person does. I've just always felt like I had more of an insatiable need than other people did. So I kind of just sought out places where I could belong. Places that needed me as much as I needed them. It takes a village to raise a child, right? I guess I just had a pretty good village."

The more he learned about Summer, the more he realized what an inner strength she had. With a mom who hadn't been present and a dad who had but had seldom been home, she probably hadn't gotten a lot of parental direction and guidance. He was impressed that she was able to figure out what she most needed and then find a way to get it. Just imagining what kind of obstacles she must've had to overcome to get to where she was now was mind blowing.

Maintaining her sense of self-worth through all of that must've been difficult, too. Or maybe she'd lost it and she'd had to fight to get it back. Regardless, he was in awe of her.

"How many kids do you want?"

He chuckled. "Well, I can't say that the number *ten* ever crossed my mind even once before now— a lot of times, I thought my family's five was too much. I guess I just always wanted what felt right."

But honestly, he was thinking that three or so would probably be what felt right. As he looked out at the beautiful surroundings with an incredible woman at his side, he worried that he might not be good enough for her in a lot more ways than just not wanting as many kids as she did. He had plenty of areas in his life where he strove to be perfect but was so far from it that he worried he might never get it right.

Chapter Fifteen

SUMMER

As Summer walked across campus toward the Student Center, she saw Avery walking from a sidewalk that joined Summer's, and she stopped and waited for her to catch up.

They started walking side by side and Avery asked, "How are things going in the Welcome Center?"

Summer felt like she lost a couple of inches in height just thinking about it and exhaled a huge breath. "I am so glad it's Friday. This week has been at least three weeks long."

"It's Thursday."

Summer just stared at Avery for a long moment. "I don't even know how that's possible."

"It's going that good, huh? I've noticed that everyone

on your side of the wall has been getting more and more stressed as the week goes on."

"It's a mess. The number of new applicants just isn't where it should be for this time of year, so the Assistant VP of Enrollment Management is breathing down Tess's neck, so she has put the pressure on us all. I know we get to this point every single year, and it always makes us stress out. How are things going in Admissions?"

"I hate to say it, but we aren't quite as busy as we usually are at this time of year. Two or three of our student employees have called in sick or too busy with homework every day, and we've been just fine without them."

Summer shook her head. "So we really are behind. We've been emailing prospective students, Everett has other companies emailing out for us, Brock has been finding even more companies to donate scholarships to entice more students, Elle has been busy with open houses, all of our on-location recruiters are in high schools every single day. They're even doing lunches with students whose counselors say they're interested. Pavani and I are in the schools in our recruitment area as much as we can be and still get our jobs here done. It doesn't seem like there's much more we can do and still survive."

Summer opened the door to the Student Center and they both walked through.

"Some years are just like that," Avery said. "But the numbers will be there when you need them."

Summer let out a long breath. "I needed your kind of optimism today, Avery. Thank you." As they neared the doors to the Welcome Center, she said, "I've actually got three students with some unique circumstances I wanted to talk with you about. Mind if I follow you to your desk?"

"You can under one condition," she said, pulling open the door to Admissions. "You give me an update on you and Brock."

The change in emotions she felt going from work stress to thinking of Brock was so abrupt it actually made her laugh. "Well, we've seen each other practically every day after work for the past two weeks. I'm to the point where every time anyone says anything, I relate it to Brock —he's at the front of my thoughts that much."

Avery said, "Aww, that's so sweet!" as she sat down at her desk.

Summer peeked over the top of the half wall before she sat in the chair beside Avery's desk, making sure none of her coworkers could hear, especially Brock. "It's bad, Avery. Valeria knew I was having a super stressful week, so when I was in the shower this morning, she went out and got us each one of 'The Everything' breakfasts from Moose on the Loose. When I opened the box, I actually said, 'Look at these hash browns, especially here at the top —don't they remind you of Brock's intentionally messy hair?' Valeria has officially declared me a hopeless case."

"I think it's adorable. What have you got for me?"

Summer brought up her email on her phone and gave Avery the information on all three students. While Avery was doing her thing, Summer noticed Brock get up from his office and walk toward Summer's. When he didn't see her there, he turned around and spotted her at Avery's desk, then mouthed, *I'll talk to you after*. She smiled and gave him a nod.

"And," Avery said, dragging out the word as her fingers flew across her keyboard before pressing *Enter* with a flourish, "all three are taken care of!"

"Avery, you are magic. Thank you."

Avery turned in her chair so she faced Summer and studied her for a moment, and Summer tried to make sure she appeared happy and normal. But either Summer was failing at it or Avery was ultra-perceptive, because she said, "You don't quite seem yourself. I mean, I get that you're stressed from work, but it feels like it's something beyond that. Are you okay?"

Summer smiled and perked herself up more, just like she always did. "Yep!" Then she remembered what Brock had told her about not being responsible for everyone else's happiness and that she was allowed to feel her feelings.

So she decided to take a chance and feel her feelings in front of Avery. "Okay, maybe there is something." Or maybe she didn't want to even think about the feelings. But Avery was looking at her with a concerned expression, so maybe it was too late to go back. She took a big breath and let it out slowly, hoping it would calm her heart that had started racing.

"I'm spending enough time with Brock that things are just naturally getting more serious. And I'm scared, Avery. I've never gotten to this point with a guy before. I always end things long before this. But Brock is just different from every other guy, so I really don't want any of it to end. But I'm also so afraid of continuing forward because it's all such unknown territory. I really don't want to mess it up, but I have no idea what I'm doing. Or if I can handle it."

"You can handle it and you're not going to mess it up."

"How do you know that?"

"Because I know you, and you're awesome."

Avery leaned forward and gave Summer a hug, which she apparently needed way more than she could've guessed. But Avery's words of confidence in Summer's abilities didn't actually comfort her, because she didn't believe them.

"Summer?"

Tess's voice came from the other side of the half wall. She quickly let go of Avery's hug, blinking a few times to make sure her eyes weren't going to look like they might be teary, and turned to her boss. "Yeah?"

"When you get done here, do you mind meeting with me in my office?"

Summer nodded and said goodbye to Avery. She felt

her phone buzz and looked down at it to see that she'd gotten a text from her dad.

DAD: Hi, sunshine! Just wanted to pop in and say that I hope you have a great day.

She smiled and sent him a *Thank you! I needed that* message back, then went through the gap in the wall to the Welcome Center side. She looked but didn't see Brock as she walked through the common area of their offices and back to Tess's office.

Tess eyed her as she sat down. "Are you doing okay?"

Summer put on her happy, peppy face. "Yep!" She might let herself feel her feelings for a quick moment with Avery, but she wasn't about to with her boss. "What did you want to talk with me about?"

"We had a decent number of applicants after the Aquamoose Tracks event a few weeks ago, which was great, especially considering the sprinkler incident. So I think the one we do at the end of this month will go well after implementing the tweaks we talked about.

"I just wanted to check in to see how you feel about the presentation you've been giving at high school events and to brainstorm with you about anything else we can do to get our numbers up. We're at midterms now, and I'd hate to see us head into the second half of the semester with the numbers still coming in at the same pace that they are."

By the time they had finished brainstorming all the things that could be done to bring in more student applications, Summer was feeling more mentally numb and lightheaded than ever. Maybe she could handle showing just a tiny bit of her feelings around her boss because she really needed advice, and it was the only way she could ask.

She looked down at her notes. "There's just more work here than I could ever possibly get to, and I'm having a hard time knowing where to even start."

"I suggest putting all your notes into a list, then give each one a score on how big of an impact it'll make. Then look at the scores to decide where your time is going to be best spent."

Tess leaned forward in her chair, her elbows on the table, her hands almost reaching across to Summer, like she wanted her words to zing across the desk to her more fully. "That's the hard thing about good things—there are always multiple good things out there, and choosing one often means not choosing another. So make sure you're taking the time to stop and think about whether you're okay with that before making your choice."

Summer nodded, thanked Tess, picked up her notes, and headed out of Tess's office.

And, because she automatically related anything

anyone said to Brock, she thought about how the very nature of a serious relationship—one that seemed to be getting more serious every day—was all about choosing one person over all others. From about the time she'd been old enough to get her driver's license, she'd started to notice how difficult it was for her to commit to choosing plans to do one thing over another. How could she commit to a serious relationship when the consequences could affect the rest of her entire life? She definitely didn't feel qualified to make that kind of choice.

As soon as she got to her office, Brock knocked on her doorframe, a winning smile on his face. "Good morning. How's the stress level?"

"Oh, you know. On a scale of one to ten, somewhere around twenty-seven. How about yours?"

"I've gotten mine down to about twenty-five, so I'm thinking of celebrating."

"You definitely should. Hey, listen, I don't think we better get together tonight; Tess just loaded on more work, and I think I better stay focused on getting it under control."

He paused, studying her, then nodded. "Okay. Let me know if you change your mind, or if you get hungry this evening and want me to bring some food."

"Thank you."

"Are you still good to go with me to my family get-together tomorrow?"

She pasted on her happy, peppy face and said, "Of course! I wouldn't miss it!" Then she reached for his hand and gave it a quick squeeze. "I better get focused on work."

As soon as he walked out of her office, she closed the door behind him. After taking a few deep breaths, she headed over to her desk and buried herself in work.

Chapter Sixteen

BROCK

"**A**re you ready for this?" Brock asked as he and Summer walked from his truck around to the back of his parents' house. The weather had turned cooler the last few days, and he was definitely glad they had both worn jackets.

"Am I excited to meet the people who grew up with you and are probably willing to share all the best stories about you? You bet I am. Are *you* ready for this?"

"I think I'm even less ready now," he joked. But a big part of him wasn't joking. He was feeling a lot of the same restlessness and tightening in his chest that he had felt when he was a kid bringing a friend over to his house for the first time. Of course, his siblings had all grown up and weren't nearly as chaotic now. They were all pretty cool, actually. But he hadn't ever cared as much about a woman as he did about Summer, so it amped up everything he felt. He really wanted them to like her and her to like them.

Summer was carrying a big bowl of the pasta salad she'd made, even though he hadn't said that they needed to bring anything and was impressed she'd thought of it. As soon as his mom saw them walk around the back, she came rushing forward from where she'd been setting food on a table, waving his dad to follow. Her dark hair was up in a bun, the gray at the front weaving through the mess of a bun like a ribbon. His dad's hair was in need of a haircut, as usual, his dark gray and black hair at the back of his neck curling around.

"Mom, this is Summer. Summer, this is my mom, Robin, and my dad, Jeff."

His mom grabbed the salad from Summer, handed it off to Brock's brother, then wrapped her arms around Summer. "Oh, it's so good to meet you! Brock told me he was bringing a woman that he'd been dating, but I had no idea you'd be so beautiful!"

Summer turned to Brock. "Just so you know, I love your mom."

His mom laughed and said, "Aren't you the sweetest. And thank you for bringing whatever's in that bowl. Oh goodness, I'm still wearing my apron. How embarrassing. I probably got flour on your shirt, too—oh, look, I did." She reached forward and attempted to brush it off.

"It's fine, Robin. It just makes me look like I did more work than I did."

His dad reached a hand out and shook Summer's. "It's been a long time since Brock's brought a woman to a family dinner, even though we've all been begging him to for years. You'll have to forgive us if we get a little too excited."

Brock could feel his cheeks heating up already. Knowing his family, he should probably get used to the sensation. He gave his glasses a nudge back up.

"Well, I'm going to go get this apron off and grab the rolls. My hair is probably a fright—I should check that, too. You all get introduced and chatting and I'll be back out in a bit."

Brock turned to his siblings, who were all standing by their spouses near the tables, looking like they might introduce themselves any second if he didn't introduce them first.

"Everyone, this is Summer Graham." They all waved. He motioned to his sister and her husband, who had been in a wheelchair for as long as he'd known him. "Summer, this is my sister, Alyssa, and her husband, Spencer. That little guy on his lap is Zachary. He's what? Six months old now?"

Alyssa nodded. "Yep! And that little blonde girl in the sandbox is our two-year-old, Gracie."

Then he motioned to his other sister. "And this is

April—she and Alyssa are twins. She and Max got married last fall, and they're expecting a baby at Christmastime. And this is my youngest brother, Hudson, and his wife, Fiona. They're both in grad school at LBSU. And this is my other brother, Rylan, and his wife, Lara. Lara is also pregnant, and she's due right at the beginning of the year."

Lara reached over and gave April a fist bump. Brock motioned at them. "They're only a little excited that they'll be having kids so close to the same age."

He glanced at Summer, wondering what she thought of his constantly growing family. She was her usual charming, friendly self, and was already hugging all of them and saying how great it was to meet them and started chatting with them all and asking them questions about themselves.

As his dad manned the grill and Hudson and Fiona both went inside to help his mom bring the last of the dinner items outside, he took Summer on a little tour of his backyard, showing her the places he used to play as a kid.

When they were a bit away from his family, Summer asked, "How old are your siblings again?"

"My sisters are twenty-five, Rylan is twenty-four, and Hudson is twenty-three."

"Wow. So we're both older than all of them, and they're all married."

Brock nodded. "And three are already having kids. So, yeah, I'm the odd man out. I think that they've been worried that I'm so far behind and I'll never find love. It'd definitely be easier to be at family dinners if I was married, too, but I love them and I love getting together with them."

"They all live close?"

He nodded. "They all graduated from Lake Baldwin State, and they all live in the tri-town area."

Summer glanced back over at them and said, "That's really sweet."

By the time they were all ready to eat, the chicken was overcooked, which was fine—it was the way Brock had gotten used to eating it when he was a kid—and everyone loaded their plates up with all the sides everyone brought.

All fifteen of them found seats at the long picnic tables in the middle of the yard and weren't too far into dinner before Summer said, "Tell me what Brock was like as a kid."

He knew the question had been inevitable, but he still cringed a bit in anticipation of his siblings' answers.

"Okay," April said, her fork in her hand, "but to understand what Brock was like, you need to understand what the rest of us were like."

"Very true," Rylan said, nodding.

"And you have to understand that there was Brock, then a four-year gap, and then there were four of us in a two-year time span."

"So our house was basically chaos, twenty-four seven," Hudson said.

"It was not chaos," Brock's mom cut in.

April looked up, considering. "Pandemonium?"

"Anarchy?" Alyssa offered.

"Oh," Hudson said, "I've got it. Bedlam."

"Okay, fine, it was chaotic," his mom said. But then turning to Summer, she added, "Please remember, dear, the part about giving birth to four kids in a two-year time span."

Summer smiled. "The fact that you even survived their first few years of life speaks volumes about you."

Brock's mom beamed.

"Anyway," April continued, "our house was constantly a mess. And not just a little cluttered. Whatever you're imagining right now, double it. Or triple it. Maybe quadruple. I think it would've taken a dozen adults to clean the house as quickly as we messed it up. And we were very rambunctious kids.

"When Alyssa and I were about five, our dad finished the big room above the garage." She pointed at the garage and the windows they could see from where they were sitting. "He said if we wanted, we could use it as a playroom or as a bedroom and all of us could sleep in there. Of course, that sounded like it was just about the coolest thing ever, so we all moved up into that room instead of being crowded into two bedrooms in the rest of the house."

"But it was our playroom, too," Rylan said. "I mean they didn't exactly say we couldn't, so we hauled tons of stuff up there, too."

"But not Brock," April said. "He chose to stay in one of the old bedrooms by himself."

"Tell me I didn't get the best deal out of all of us," Brock said. But every one of his siblings just shrugged, like they didn't actually think he did, which kind of baffled him. He glanced at Summer and saw her smiling, soaking in every bit of what they were saying.

"I think we liked the chaos," Hudson said. "Maybe even craved it. I have great memories of the four of us in that big bedroom."

Alyssa chuckled. "We used to always joke that since Brock was born first, he got first dibs on the 'need to be good'— a good son, a good student, a good person—and took every last bit of it, leaving the rest of us with none of it."

"You missed out on all the fun," April said. "But you should've seen Brock's room. Everywhere in the house was a mess of chaos and noise, and Brock's bedroom was a pristine oasis polluted by neither noise nor clutter, not even the tiniest speck of dust."

"She's not exaggerating," Rylan said. "You could peek in there at any time of day, and his bed would be made with everything tucked in exactly, his chair neatly under his desk, everything completely organized."

Hudson nodded. "And of course, the only way it stayed that way was because he didn't let any of us in there."

"Oh," Rylan said, "but the best part was when he would bring a friend over for the first time. As they were walking through the chaos of our house to get to his haven of a room, Brock would walk with his eyes straight forward, head not turning at all, like if he didn't look at all the mess around him, the friend wouldn't see it, either.

"But of course, the friend would actually be looking around, face full of shock, their jaw dropped. After that first time, they acted more normal as they made the trek back to Brock's room."

"I always wished we could be in there," Alyssa said. "You know, so we could see their reaction when a friend walked into his room for the first time after seeing the rest of our house."

Summer was laughing now, even wiping away laughing tears from her lower lashes. Brock, on the other hand, still felt like his face was going to remain in a constant state of heat all night long.

"I'll have you know," Brock's mom said, "that it wasn't always that way."

"True," Hudson said. "We were a ton less chaotic by about the time we were in middle school."

"So about the time I moved out and went to college," Brock said.

His mom nodded. "These monkeys all grew up and got cleaner and calmer as they did. And every one of them has clean houses now."

Little Gracie, who had been silently dipping a carrot in an obscene amount of ranch dressing, licking it off, then dipping it again, suddenly talked in her cute little voice. "Gramma, no looking at my room right now, 'kay?"

And on and on the stories went. The more embarrassed Brock got, the more it fueled his siblings. But Summer seemed to love them all.

Then his brother Rylan said, "But remember that one time when I was like six and went into your room when you weren't home and drew all over your walls?"

"I remember," Brock said. "It was with a green marker. I think you were trying to draw a mural of the entire town."

"I'm pretty sure I finished three of the walls before anyone caught me." Rylan was laughing so much that he could barely understand him when he said, "You were so mad! I'm pretty sure you hated me for an entire year after that!"

"For the record, it wasn't nearly that long."

Brock looked over at Summer, expecting to see her laughing as much as she had been with all their other stories, but she wasn't. The smile on her face wasn't a real smile—he was getting very good at being able to tell when it was a fake. He would've guessed something was up anyway, though, by the way she wasn't quite making eye contact.

But then his dad went over to the fire pit and used the

hook tool to pull the lid off a Dutch oven and said, "The peach cobbler's ready!"

The smell of it wafted over to their tables, and it was all anyone could talk about. Things were a little loud as everyone got bowls of Brock's favorite dessert dished up and ice cream scooped on top, but everyone quieted as they started eating. He leaned in close to Summer. "Are you okay?"

She smiled widely. "Yep! Your family is so much fun."

But he couldn't shake the feeling that everything wasn't okay.

Chapter Seventeen

Summer was in her bathroom, getting ready to go to the Saturday night tri-town meet-up, directly across the hall from where Valeria was getting ready in her bathroom. It was nearly seven, which meant that it had been almost twenty-four hours since she'd had dinner with Brock's family. So that also meant that she'd had plenty of time to get over the new fears that had presented themselves.

Except she hadn't gotten over them. In fact, they seemed to be multiplying as the day went on.

She turned around and leaned against her counter, her powder brush still in her hand. "I just can't get the conversation out of my head when Brock's brother was telling about drawing on Brock's walls and that Brock was mad at him for a year."

Valeria's eyes flicked from where she was leaning in close, focusing on her eyes as she applied eyeliner to meet Summer's eyes in the mirror. She finished that eye, then turned around and leaned against her own counter, facing Summer, one eye still without eyeliner.

"Brock was a kid then. He was, what, ten? Eleven? You can't really judge him for something that he did that long ago. Plus, I really doubt he hated his brother for a year. This one time, my brother Santiago went into my room when I wasn't home and poured water into every one of my shoes. Weird choice, I know. Siblings do things to bug each other—it's part of their job description. When I came home and saw it, I shouted something like 'I'm never going to forgive you in my entire life,' and I got over it in a day. Okay, maybe two."

"No, I totally get that it's something stupid and that it's not something that should even remotely matter right now. And really, I *don't* judge him for it at all. It's not about that. I know that in the grand scheme of things, this is minuscule. But as stupid as it is that I'm fixating on something that happened so long ago, I just can't stop. Things are heading toward getting very serious for us. Did I tell you that every single one of his siblings is already married?"

Valeria nodded.

"And that he's the oldest by *four years?*"

Valeria nodded again.

"And his family was all looking at me like I'm the one. And maybe I *want* to be the one. But maybe that's also terrifying."

"Why? You really like him."

Maybe it went far beyond "like." Lately, whenever she thought of him, "love" was the word that popped into her head every time.

"I know. I do. But Val, marriage isn't temporary and I know that if we stay on the path we're on, that's where we're headed. I could see it in the faces of every adult in his family. I can see it in Brock's face. And *forever* is scary."

"Why?"

"A couple of days ago, my boss was talking about choosing one good thing over another and how when you make a choice, you are closing off all other options. What if I make the wrong choice and close off all others when I really shouldn't have?"

"Do you really think you're making the wrong choice by dating Brock?"

"No, but am I even qualified to make that decision? What in my life has given me experience in that? Even you agree that everything I do is short-term. Every hobby I start, every major I've had. I haven't even kept my bedroom furniture arranged the same way for more than two months since I was six and found out that if sat with my back against the corner of my bed and pushed with all my might that I could move it."

"Okay, but you aren't that way with everything. You haven't been that way with the Welcome Center."

"But the Welcome Center will never ask me to commit to working there for life. A relationship is different. What if things change?"

"Like they did with your mom?"

"Like they did with Brock and his brother. What if things between Brock and me keep going really well and our relationship gets serious and we get engaged and then married and then someday things just changed and he stopped loving me?" Just the thought of it made her start breathing faster, her chest tightening.

"It's not going to happen like that."

"Sometimes it does and there's nothing you can do about it." She was suddenly feeling too hot, like the air was suffocating her. She started fanning her shirt.

"Would you be freaking out this much if it was someone other than Brock that we were talking about?"

"Of course not, because if it was anyone else, I wouldn't care enough to freak out. Why is it so hot and what is wrong with this air? It's like it doesn't have enough oxygen in it."

Valeria walked across the hall to Summer's bathroom. "Are you okay?"

But then there were two bodies making heat in the small space, so Summer quickly stepped around her, sucking in the cooler air in the hallway. "I'm just dizzy and my insides are ...I don't know, shaking. Am I having a panic attack? Is this what a panic attack feels like?"

Valeria put an arm around her and led her into their living room. "Maybe? Here, sit down, close your eyes, and take slow, deep breaths."

"There's no way things with Brock could be right if it's causing an anxiety attack."

"I don't think that's a good method of knowing what is the right answer. Now shh. Deep breaths."

"No, I'm canceling going with him to the tri-town meet-up tonight."

"Just keep taking those deep breaths. You can decide that when you're not so panicked. I know you wanted to show him your world and see how he fits in."

"But maybe I shouldn't be trying to do that at all. Maybe we shouldn't be in each other's worlds."

"What are you saying?"

"I don't know. That I need to take a step back or something. This is just too scary and too big." She pulled out her phone and tried to focus on the screen even though it seemed blurry. Her fingers were shaking, so it made it hard to type, but she managed to send a text to Brock saying, *I need to cancel tonight. Tomorrow, too. I just need space.*

She tossed the phone to the other end of the couch

and took the paper bag that apparently Valeria had gone into the kitchen to get. She tried to calm her breaths as she breathed into it, hoping it would calm her worried heart, too.

Chapter Eighteen

BROCK

By Sunday afternoon, Brock's mind felt like a jumbled mess that he could no longer untangle. So he grabbed his jacket and keys, got into his truck, and headed to the lake. There was something about being outside with the soft sounds of the water nearby that calmed his swirling thoughts and helped him to think more clearly. And if there was ever a time he needed exactly that, it was today.

He parked and headed down the incline to the lake. Instead of keeping to the groomed sandy beach, he headed to the weedy trail that led around it. As he walked, all the worries that he'd messed up the best thing he'd ever had in his life swirled around in his gut.

He'd texted Summer after she'd canceled on their plans to go to the tri-town meet-up and for a drive to look at fall leaves today, but she hadn't texted back. He wanted to know that she was okay. He wanted to know if she needed anything and what he could do.

But since she hadn't responded, he was just left with his own swirling thoughts.

He'd only had one girl tell him that she needed space once before—Jill—and that was during his sophomore year of high school. They'd both known that they were headed for a breakup, and those words had been her way of ending it as gently as possible.

But Summer's words didn't feel like that at all.

He crouched down and looked at the rocks on the trail. He picked out a few that were flat and smooth and smaller than his palm, then stood up. With one in his hand, he pulled his arm back and twisted his wrist just the way his dad had shown him when he was a kid, then sent the rock sailing out into the lake. The first one did a tiny little skip over the water then plunked down into the lake.

He adjusted for the second one and managed to send it skipping three times before it fell into the water. He realized that what he'd just done—trying, then adjusting and trying again—was exactly the "Ready, fire, aim" concept that Summer had told him weeks ago that had seemed so wrong at the time. He drew back his arm and sent the next one sailing and it skipped four times.

He wished he could do the same in his relationship with Summer. Try again, adjust, and do better. To figure out where things went wrong and not do that again. To be more perfect the next time around. That was always his goal in life, of course, but it meant more to him to be perfect for her. He wanted to be the kind of person who was worthy of her love.

He could tell that something at his parents' house on Friday night had bothered her, but he didn't know what, exactly. At first, he'd wondered if his family had scared her off. But Summer loved meeting new people and she was the least judgmental person he knew, so he dismissed that as the reason.

So, of course, his mind went to all the stories that were told about him. They had to have made her realize how imperfect he was and that no matter how hard he strived for perfection, he fell short and wasn't actually good enough for her.

But really, it had felt like she'd been slowly pulling away all week, long before she met his family.

He looked out at the lake, the surface shining and shimmering in the sun, the calmer parts near the shore on the far side reflecting the yellows and oranges and reds of the trees at the shore, and his mind started to feel less full.

But the absence of the swirling thoughts just made the emotions settling in his gut feel more pronounced. He and Summer had been spending so much time together that it made her absence feel more pronounced, too.

He missed her. He wanted to be near her. To talk with

her and hear her opinions about everything under the sun. To witness the way she made everyone around her feel happy. Loved. Included. Like they had come home whenever they were around her. He wanted to joke with her. To hear her laugh. To see the way her eyes crinkled whenever she thought of a great plan. To walk hand-in-hand with her. To kiss her goodnight at the end of each day.

She made him feel like he was home around her, too. And now that he knew what that was like, he didn't want to ever live without it.

He picked up another rock and sent it sailing across the lake, bouncing an incredible six times before it plunged into the lake.

That was what he wanted. A redo. A chance to make everything perfect for Summer.

Chapter Nineteen

SUMMER

For the first time in the six years she'd been an ambassador plus the three years she'd been an Admissions Recruiter, Summer walked into the Student Center building, headed for the Welcome Center, and wished she didn't have to be there.

She wasn't close to having a panic attack at any moment like she'd been on Saturday night, but she was still experiencing dizziness and a quivering stomach and didn't feel like herself at all. If only today was a day she was scheduled to do a college presentation in one of the high schools in her recruitment area. Or a day when she could just call in sick.

But the next Aquamoose Tracks was this weekend. Although many of the preparations that she and Brock had done for the first one carried through to the five others for this year, it was still a massive event and there were plenty of things that had to be done each time they put on the event. And today, she and Pavani were meeting together to go over all the last-minute things and there was no way she could miss it.

She took a deep breath, put on a smile that said everything was great and happy as usual, and walked into the Welcome Center lobby. Alejandro and Paige were behind the counter at the far end, so she asked in her most chipper voice, "Are you ready for our morning meeting?" Then they headed into the big meeting room where Jessa, McKay, and Takeshi were already waiting. Hopefully, none of them would notice the fact that this was the first time she had ever been the last to arrive.

Or that she couldn't joke around with them as usual. All she could manage was a short meeting that covered only what they needed to know to work that morning.

As they all headed out to their assigned tasks, Jessa held back. "Are you okay?"

Summer realized exactly how on edge she was when the simple question nearly choked her up. She swallowed down the emotions and nodded. "I'm good."

The look on Jessa's face told her she wasn't fooled, but instead of pushing Summer, she just gave her a quick hug and said, "I hope your day gets better."

She thanked Jessa, headed back into the lobby, and went through the doorway leading to the Welcome Center offices. Through the glass front of Brock's office, she could see that he was at his desk. She didn't make eye contact, but from the corner of her eye, she could see him sit up straighter, turn in his chair, and move a foot forward like he was about to stand up. Hopefulness seemed to color every aspect of his posture.

But when she didn't make eye contact still, his posture changed to a slump of disappointment. She wanted to go to him and grab his hand and lift him up and erase all the sadness or defeat or disappointment he felt. But the fear inside her stopped her cold and instead, she went into her own office and shut her door and felt like the world's worst person for doing it.

She turned on her laptop and the second monitor it was connected to and stared at her screens, trying to get her mind to focus on the dozens of tasks she needed to complete today. It was enough that she'd have been running all day just to get them all done on a day when she had all the focus in the world. She didn't know how she would get through today when she couldn't even figure out what the first thing should be.

She allowed herself a quick glance in Brock's direction, where she could see only his left leg through the glass. It was such a small part of him, but she was so drawn to it, like it was pulling at her heart, reminding her how much her heart felt that it belonged next to his. He really was the perfect guy.

But she didn't know how to shake the fear that she had been carrying around with her. Fear wasn't an emotion she dealt with often and if she did ever feel it, she just found friends to hang out with until the feeling went away. That wasn't going to fix the problem this time, though, and she didn't have a clue how to deal with the emotion.

Summer hadn't told Pavani what was going on with her. Pavani must've guessed that something was up, though, because even though Summer hadn't left her office a single time since that morning and even ate a lunch of a stale granola bar and a package of trail mix that she'd found at the back of one of her drawers so she didn't have to leave, Pavani came into her office at 2:00 for their meeting carefully, like she was approaching an injured animal. "You doing okay?"

She pasted her smile back on. "Yep! Let's get this thing planned!"

Smile or not, she couldn't focus on any of the things they were trying to go through. Eventually, Pavani set her pen on her tablet and leaned back in her chair, arms crossed. "Are you going to tell me what's up?"

Summer let out a slow breath. "Before Brock and I went on our first date, I told Valeria and Avery that it wouldn't be a big deal to date Brock. That we'd been friends and coworkers for so long that if we started a relationship and it ended that we'd be able to go back to being coworkers and friends, no problem. They acted like I was naive to think that." She swallowed. "It turns out that I was."

"Oh, sweetie. It's over between you and Brock?"

Summer looked down at her desk. "Not officially, no. I just don't know how to be the kind of person I need to be for it not to be over."

She heard a voice that made her sit up straight to see if she'd heard correctly. Then she stood and hurried to her door. She hadn't been hearing things—her dad had been saying hello to everyone as he headed toward her office. "Dad! What are you doing here?"

He smiled, his arms spread wide, like he was open for a hug as he walked toward her. "You didn't quite sound like yourself when we talked on the phone yesterday, and I couldn't shake the feeling that I needed to see you in person. So when I got to work this morning, I asked Pete to find me a flight and cancel my meetings and here I am."

Summer threw her arms around her dad and gave him a really long hug. She hadn't realized how badly she had needed it and didn't pull back for a very long time. When she did, there was a tear trying to escape her right eye—she hated that. She quickly batted it away.

"Are you okay?"

She shook her head. She wasn't going to tempt the tears to make a reappearance by actually using words.

Tess walked down the hall just then and saw the two of them in the doorway of Summer's office.

"Mr. Graham! Hello! It's so great to see you again. I didn't know you were coming for a visit."

"It was a bit of a surprise, even for me. Summer didn't know I was coming."

Tess's eyes landed on Summer. She didn't know what Tess saw when she looked at her—probably a mix of something resembling distress and emotional exhaustion. Then Tess glanced back at Summer's dad before meeting Summer's eyes again.

"Go with your dad. Take the rest of the day off—whatever you've got on your schedule for the rest of the day, we'll take care of it."

"Are you sure?" Summer's mind immediately went to the long list of things she needed to do. She couldn't actually think of a single thing on the list, but she knew it was hefty.

Tess nodded. "I am. Go."

So Summer left with her dad.

Chapter Twenty

BROCK

r. Graham had been popping into the Welcome Center every couple of months for the entire four years that Brock worked there. He was always pretty chatty, too—Summer must've inherited it from him—so Brock had gotten to know him pretty well. He was a good guy.

Brock had glanced in Summer's office whenever he walked out of his, and every time, she looked so sad. Since he felt like anything he tried to do would make things worse, which left him unable to help at all, he was so glad that her dad showed up today.

As Brock walked from the Welcome Center lobby to the common area, Deja looked up at him. "How are you holding up?"

Brock didn't even know how to answer that.

"Have a seat."

Brock did as he was told and sat down. "How long have you and your husband been together?"

"Three glorious years."

"Did you ever need space while you were dating?"

"Me? Heavens no."

"Oh."

"But my husband sure did, bless his heart. It was before we got engaged. He had a little freak-out and was outta there faster than a hot knife through butter."

"So what do you do when that happens? Because right now I'm doing nothing and that's about the hardest thing to do."

"Well, I suppose it depends on the person and what they need."

"How do I find out what she needs?"

"You could ask her."

He shook his head. "You saw her today. I don't think she wants to talk to me at all. If she wants me to give her space, then of course I'll honor her wishes. But if she wants me to fight for her, I want her to know that I'm willing to do anything."

Deja looked at him for a long moment, then she said, "You're one of the truly good guys. You know that, right?"

His worries were deep and fierce, but Deja's words were like a bucket of water thrown on a raging fire. It didn't come close to putting it out and would likely be just as big a few minutes later, but it helped. "I don't know. It kind of just feels like I failed."

"Have you given this relationship your all?"

"I think I have."

"Then you haven't failed. And you should listen to me because I'm..."

Brock smiled. "Right, again."

"Yep. It's there in my name. Do you love her?"

"I haven't told her yet, but yes. I really do."

"Do you get along with her?"

He let out a single breath of a chuckle. "So much better than I thought I would. I always thought I needed to only date other perfectionists or rule-followers or planners so I wouldn't annoy them by being that way myself."

"And how did that work out for you?"

"Not great. We always clashed. It amazes me how easygoing Summer is, even with those parts of me I thought she would hate."

"That's because the two of you balance out each other's strengths and weaknesses. And lemme tell you what else. People aren't perfect and shouldn't be expected to be. Yourself included. Accept that. Know that doing your best is all you need to be doing.

"That goes for love, too. Things don't need to be perfect—you don't need to be, she doesn't need to be. Two imperfect people can come together perfectly and it'll make both of them better than they were."

"You're a pretty wise person, Deja."

"I keep telling you all that. You should listen to me more."

"Definitely." He smiled, then pulled his phone out of his pocket when it buzzed. He looked down at the screen, confused.

"Is that something you need to deal with?"

"It's an email from Summer's roommate." He swiped to open the message.

FROM: valeria.ramos@lakebaldwinstate.edu
TO: brock.mcmillan@lakebaldwinstate.edu
SUBJECT: Our girl Summer

I have information that I feel is important to share with you. I don't have a class right now. Can you chat? If so, let me know, and I'll meet you halfway between my building and yours.

Valeria

"She wants to meet and give me insider information."

"Then go man, go! Start fighting for Summer!"

Brock replied to Valeria's email with a quick, *I'm*

heading toward you right now, stood up and thanked Deja, then hurried out of the building.

He had seen Valeria enough times over the past few weeks and from her coming into the Welcome Center countless times over the years to recognize her from quite a distance in the crowd of students walking across campus. Seeing her felt like a lifeline had just been thrown out to him as he was drowning at sea.

He thanked her for meeting with him, but she didn't waste any time on pleasantries and got straight to business.

"Are you worried that Summer is no longer interested in you?"

He rubbed at the corner of his eyebrow, then nudged his glasses up. "Yeah."

"*Lo siento*, I was worried that's what was going to happen! Okay, listen up. She hasn't backed off because of a lack of interest."

It felt like a giant weight was lifted from his chest and he could suddenly breathe easier.

"It's because of an overabundance of fear."

"Fear?"

"You know..." Valeria waved her hand. "Fear of commitment. Of whether or not you'll always love her and be there for her. Which, given her background, I think we can agree is understandable. And given all that I know of *you*, which I've got to say, is considerable—our girl really likes to talk about you—you are going to know what to do with that information."

"I think I do." His whole body felt so much lighter than it had before. "I don't know how I can ever thank you enough."

Valeria shrugged. "I find that homemade guacamole is an excellent way to say thank you."

"You've got it," Brock said, already turning back toward the Student Center. "I've got to go!" And then he took off running.

Chapter Twenty-One

SUMMER

If Summer had to go back and choose all over again, she would still choose to move to a neighboring state to go to college, and she would still choose to stay living there after graduation. She needed that distance for a lot of reasons. And maybe one of the biggest reasons was that instead of having expectations of her dad being around and then being let down, she got to fully appreciate and enjoy every single visit she got with him.

Because she was *so* glad to see her dad. She had needed his calming presence so badly. He had taken her to the campus ice cream shop, where they served the one and only Aquamoose Tracks—the flavor he got no matter what. It was the first place they always went whenever he visited, and she felt the comfort in that routine.

As they ate their ice cream (lemon cheesecake for her, as usual), they chatted about random things. What her mom was up to (just got back from volunteering at a turtle conservation in Sri Lanka), how work was going for her (the second Aquamoose Tracks of the year was in a few days), how work was going for him (busy as ever, but not too busy to fly to see her), and how beautiful the fall leaves were. It was nice to get her mind on other more normal things. For a minute, she even managed to forget about her roiling stomach and swirling head and the hurt in her heart.

But the pain and the knowledge and the fear were always waiting for the slightest opportunity to come back out.

They had both finished their ice cream a while ago. Her dad pushed his empty bowl aside and folded his arms, leaning on the table. "So are you going to talk about what's really bothering you?"

She glanced around at the reason she hadn't already brought it up—all the people that were close enough that they might catch the conversation. Even if they couldn't hear, they'd still be close enough to see the distress on her face.

Her dad nodded. "What do you say we get out of here? Where do you want to go?"

"How about the lake? I have some camp chairs in my trunk."

He chuckled. "I don't doubt that. I think if there was a catastrophic natural disaster in the area, the Red Cross would come to you first because you might just have everything anyone needed right in your trunk."

"Hey, you never know when you might need a half a dozen decks of cards or a picnic blanket or a couple of Gatorades. Come on—I'll drive."

Once she parked her car, they each slung a camp chair over a shoulder and headed down to the lake. Outside of campus, the lake was her favorite place to be. It was a place of friends and fun and people supporting each other. A place of gathering and excitement and games and love and music and nature all in one place. Even when, like now, the place was virtually empty, she still felt its presence.

"Do you want to walk barefoot in the water?"

Summer pulled her jacket a little tighter. "Dad, the water is probably freezing."

"But you still want to?"

She wasn't about to ask her dad to take off his shoes and socks and get his feet in the lake at this time of year, even though it was her favorite thing.

He must've sensed her need, though, because he slid the camp chair off his shoulder and onto the sand, then started to take off his shoes and socks and roll up his pant legs. So she grinned and did the same. "You really are the best. Thanks, Dad."

They both yelped as they stepped into the freezing water, and she hoped her feet would be numbed to the cold soon. Even as cold as it was, she could immediately feel tension and stress spilling out of her as they walked, the sand pushing up between her toes. There was just something about walking in water over sand that grounded her like nothing else.

"Did Mom want to come with you?" It had been so many years since she'd asked that question. She hadn't even realized it was on her mind at all until it popped out.

He paused a moment before shaking his head. "She needed to recover from jet lag and said she'd been on a plane too recently."

Summer had perfected not getting upset about answers like that a long time ago. She should've known to not even ask.

"Listen, sunshine, there are some things that I've felt like I should talk with you about for a while."

They walked a few more steps in silence, maybe while he was figuring out how he was going to say what he wanted to say. Then he headed over to their camp chairs, pulled them out of their cases, and set them upright at the water's edge. They both took a seat, and she played in the sand with her toes under the shallow water as she waited for him to continue.

Eventually, he took a deep breath and said, "Not everyone is cut out to be a mom. Even beyond that, your mom has some pretty big issues that she's had to grapple with over the years. And those issues have absolutely nothing to do with you." He said each word slowly, dragging it out in emphasis.

On the surface, she knew that. It wasn't the first time she'd heard it. But it was the first time his words had entered so deeply into her heart, sinking their way right into her core. It was the first time she realized how much she hadn't really believed it ever before. At least not fully.

"With as little as me and your mom were home while you were growing up, I hired a bunch of people to help. Do you remember Charlie, the groundskeeper?"

She nodded.

"And Jules and Reina were maids."

"And Melissa."

"Oh yeah! I forgot about her. And then there were your nannies."

Summer nodded. "Zora, Morgan, Jenny, and then Natalie."

"I remember when you were a little girl and you used to do Summergrahams for all of them. Do you remember those?"

She laughed. "Yeah. I did one about six weeks ago, actually."

"Why does that not surprise me? You're always so good at looking out for everyone's feelings. I wish I had been around more to look out for your feelings." He paused for a moment. "All those people, though, Summer? Your nannies, the people helping with the yard and the house? They were paid to do *a job*. They weren't paid to love you. But oh, how they all loved you. Everybody you came into contact with loved you."

A tear fell from her eye and ran down her cheek and she didn't even care.

"Then, of course, there came a time when you got old enough that you didn't need a nanny anymore. But that was at an age when you still needed parents." He reached out and gave her hand a squeeze. "I'm sorry I didn't understand that well enough back then. And I'm sorry that everyone I brought into your life to love you was only temporary. I should've been around more. I wish I would've understood back then just how important family is."

"I really wished I could've had you around a lot more, too. But the truth is, Dad, I forgave you for not being around a long time ago." As soon as she said the words, though, she started questioning them. She had consciously forgiven him. But had her subconscious fully gotten the memo? Or was she still subconsciously rebelling against what he wanted for her? She was going to have to think more about that sometime.

He gave her hand another squeeze before he let go again. They both sat in silence, looking at the edge of the water as it gently washed over her feet and lapped at the shore.

"So, based on what little I saw in the Welcome Center, I'm guessing that your tough time right now has to do with you and Brock?"

Summer nodded. "What if I don't have what it takes to be in a serious relationship?"

He placed his hands in his lap. "I can't offer you any great relationship advice, but I can tell you what I know about *you*. You love fiercely and fully and you're one of the most loyal people I know. You genuinely care about others and want what's best for them. I can't imagine any qualities that are needed more in a long-term relationship than that. If anyone has what it takes, it's you."

She swallowed the emotion welling up inside her. Did she really have what it took? Her dad might not have been around nearly enough, but he never once lied to her. So maybe she did have what it took and she never knew it.

"Were you scared to death when your's and Mom's relationship first started getting really serious?"

"Oddly enough, no. But this isn't about me. Tell me what's making you scared."

She took a breath and decided to just spill it all. "Okay. Well, I guess some people might say that I have a fear of commitment." She paused a moment. "Okay, several people said it. But it doesn't really feel like that to me. It's more that I'm afraid of closing off all other possibilities and being worried that maybe I made the wrong decision and I shouldn't have.

"And then, I guess I'm worried about the possibility that I won't feel loved somewhere down the road. Or what if he isn't always there for me? Mom committed to loving me when she had me, then she decided she wanted different things out of life. What if Brock decided later that he wanted different things?"

Her dad seemed to ponder for a few moments, then said, "Remember when you were little and you'd start screaming in the middle of the night that there was a spider on your ceiling? I would come running in and turn on the light, and there would be nothing there. Then you'd realize that it had just been a nightmare and there hadn't actually been anything to worry about."

"Except that one time when there was."

"Yes, except that one time when there was. I'm going to ask you some questions and I want you to really think about your answers. It'll be like turning on the light, and shining a light on a problem is always the best way to figure out how to deal with it. Because if you do, you'll either see that there's something there to be afraid of and how big it is —like that one time when there actually was a spider on your ceiling—or it'll help you to see that there's nothing there at all and you don't have anything to be afraid of."

Summer nodded. "I like that plan."

"Okay, first question. And think back to everything you know about Brock. Does he normally give up on things after a little while?"

The sun was getting lower and lower on the horizon as she ran her toes through the water and the sand as she thought of all of the work projects she'd seen him face over the years. Tess would assign the team goals or Brock would set them for himself—ridiculously large goals at times. And he never gave up on any of them, no matter how hard they got.

"He doesn't. He decided he wanted to be the Assistant Director over Financial Aid when he was a student. There weren't any openings in the Welcome Center when he graduated, though, so he went to academic advising for three years until he could become an admissions recruiter. And he did that until the position he wanted was open. I asked him where he thought he'd be in five years, and he said doing the same job because he felt so passionately about it."

Her dad smiled. "He sounds like a pretty dedicated person. Does he ever slack on the job?"

"No. Even if the rest of us do."

"So, given what you know of him, do you think that sometimes he won't be there for you?"

Okay, now that he was spelling everything out for her, it seemed ridiculous that she'd ever been afraid that he might not. He was always there for anyone who needed him. She shook her head.

"Does Brock understand how important family is?"

For years, she'd been hearing stories about Brock's family, and there was always an undercurrent of love beneath everything he said. She realized that knowledge had always let her know that she could trust him, even when they had been disagreeing about so many things while working together for years. She had grown up in a family where *family* hadn't seemed important, and she'd admired how important family had seemed to him long before she'd been attracted to him.

"He does. He has four siblings he helped to raise, and even though they're very different from him, he loves them a lot."

Her dad's smile seemed to have a breath of relief behind it. "Okay, then, one last question, and this one is more about you, I guess. You mentioned worrying about closing off all other possibilities—do you think there might be someone out there who would be a better fit for you than Brock?"

She shook her head as she looked out at the brilliant colors of the sunset and thought of her and Brock watching a similar sunset during the football game back when this all started. "Honestly, until I started dating Brock, I didn't know there was a guy out there who was as perfect for me as he is. I think maybe down deep I knew that, and it was what scared me the most."

It hit her how her friends had been saying exactly that all along—that it was her fear that would stop something great happening between her and Brock. She hadn't realized how right they'd been until now.

And then the full weight of the knowledge of her realizations hit her with an incredible sense of urgency. A need to make things right and to do it now. "So, basically, what you're saying is I've been pushing away the guy who's perfect for me."

"It sounds like it."

"But Dad, what if he doesn't think that I'm in it fully? That I'm not ready to stick with him forever? Everyone always expects me to move on to other things quickly because that's what I do with everything outside of the Welcome Center." She could feel her words coming out in a rush, but she couldn't slow them down. "I need to find a way to convince him that I'm not going to move on."

She pulled her feet out of the water to brush the sand off, but then immediately gave up. Her shoes weren't close by anyway—she'd have to walk barefoot to her car to get a towel from her trunk. She closed up her camp chair, but the need to rush made it difficult for her to get it to slide into its sleeve.

Her dad took it from her hands and slid it in so easily. Then he put a hand on her arm. "Sunshine, this guy sounds like he's a rock. I don't think he's going to go away if you don't get to him in the next couple of minutes."

"I know, I just"—She ran her hands through her hair and glanced toward her car—"I don't want to waste another minute not being with him."

He nodded and said, "I understand."

She sprinted up the incline and across the wooden platform with the tables and up the few wooden stairs to the parking lot and pulled a towel from her trunk and raced it back down to where her dad now had both chairs folded in their sleeves and slung over his shoulder and was standing by their shoes.

Once they had their shoes on and everything back in the car and were heading toward Lake Baldwin State, Summer called Deja's cell phone. When she answered, Summer asked, "Are you still at work?"

"I am."

"Oh, good! I didn't think anyone would be this late. Is Brock still there?"

Her "yes" sounded pretty hesitant, so Summer said, "Keep him there, whatever it takes. It's important."

"Summer, what is up?"

"I need to let him know that I choose him. Always."

"Oh, my goodness sakes, this is so exciting! What do you have in mind?"

"I don't know, because I just figured everything out and there's no time, so I only have the stuff in my trunk to work with. I have a picnic blanket, so maybe I can have a picnic with him in the big meeting room. I have matches and newspapers and firewood, but no candles. Oh! I do have a couple of flashlights, though, so maybe I can use them as candles. But I have no food."

"Elle and Everett are still here. I'll have them run down to Aquamoose Crossing and get you some food for your picnic."

"Elle and Everett are still there, too?" Wow. Apparently, today was a really bad day to leave early. "Tell them thank you. I'll be there in a few minutes."

"This is all so cute, I can't even stand it! See you soon!"

It wasn't long before she and her dad were pulling into the faculty parking lot at Lake Baldwin State. When they got out of the car, she wanted to sprint the length of campus that was between her and the Welcome Center, but she needed to do something else first.

She turned to her dad and wrapped her arms around him. "Thank you for being so good at shining the light. I'm even more grateful for you now than I was as a kid afraid of a spider on my ceiling." She smiled. "And I was pretty darn grateful back then."

"You're welcome. Thank you for being you, and for always letting me into your life, even though I was so bad at it when you were younger." He tightened his squeeze before he pulled back and glanced down. "Now, do you want to maybe unroll your pant legs before we go find him?"

She couldn't believe that she could've missed something like that. She unrolled her jeans and brushed the sand off them, straightening them as she went, then grabbed the blanket and flashlights from her trunk before heading toward the Student Center. Avery was waiting for them at the doors, holding one open.

"Avery! You're here still, too?"

"Yes. I wanted to help."

The halls were partially darkened now, and as they walked down them, she said to Avery, "Oh, hey, I almost forgot to ask you. How did your date go this weekend? Was it fun?"

Avery shrugged. "It was kind of boring, actually." She glanced over at Summer. "You've helped me to realize that I need more adventure in my life."

Summer smiled and gave her friend a one-armed hug as they walked. "You'll find the right guy."

Avery turned to Summer's dad. "The last time we snuck down these halls when they were dark—well, darker than this—Summer got us out of being arrested."

Her dad threw her a questioning look, but Summer just waved it off.

When they neared the Welcome Center, Deja pushed open the door to the darkened lobby and held it open for them. Summer's attention was immediately taken inside the lobby. String lights, the same kind of lights that they had danced under when they had gone to Lookout Hill, lit the way from the ambassadors' desk down the hall toward the big meeting room.

"What is all this?" Summer asked.

Deja just shrugged. "We all just wanted to help make it special."

Everett was standing at the corner between the hallway and the lobby, and he took the blanket and flashlights from her arms and walked ahead of her to the meeting room. When she got there, Everett was spreading out the blanket and setting up the flashlights, and Elle was pouring a massive armful of packaged treats on the blanket.

Summer took a deep breath and pulled out her phone. "Okay, I'm going to text Brock and see if he can come in here."

"No need," Everett said. "It's taken care of—he'll be in here in just a moment."

She glanced behind her and saw Avery and her dad and Deja smiling and moving to the back of the room where Pavani and her husband, Zain, stood, all giving her encouraging thumbs-up as Elle and Everett joined them. And then Elle pulled out her phone and started recording, even though this didn't seem like a video-worthy moment.

Summer smiled at her dad and her work family, all standing together. "It's kind of weird to have you all in here as I profess my love to the man I've apparently been waiting my entire life for. But it also feels kind of right, too."

"I'm glad you feel that way, honey," Deja said. "Because we really don't want to leave."

Summer took a slow, calming breath as she turned to face the door, hoping it would help slow her racing heart as she waited for the man she loved to walk through the door.

Chapter Twenty-Two

BROCK

Brock ran his hands through his hair and took one last look at his computer screen and the error saying that the file he'd been working on couldn't be opened. He knew from talking with Valeria that Summer was worried about whether he would always love her and be there for her. Over time, she would know that he would just by his actions. But he wanted to do something that would help alleviate those fears *now*, so he asked Tess if he could have the rest of the afternoon off and did the one thing he could think of—make a video.

He had filmed a bunch of clips of things he had in his apartment that Summer had seen but hadn't known the story behind. Things that he had kept for years, or sometimes decades, that meant a lot to him. He knew that *things* staying important to him over a long period of time wasn't a direct correlation to *her* staying important to him forever, and it was all probably rather cheesy, but he'd filmed it anyway.

Then he filmed a bunch of clips where he'd held an object that represented something they did together and talked about what it had meant to him and how it had made him fall more fully for her. He'd held one of the pamphlets they'd given the students after the campus tour and talked about how watching her in her element helped him realize that there was a deep, vibrant side of her that he hadn't known existed before and how intrigued it made him.

He'd performed the small bit of the song and dance he'd accidentally seen her do in her Summergraham for Pavani when they'd visited her in the hospital, even though he couldn't really pull it off and felt ridiculous doing it, and talked about how it helped him to realize how much she cared for others. He held up one of the jump ropes he'd gone back to Taheny's Toys to get, and told about how it gave him a small glimpse into how strong she was, and how much it inspired him to be less rigid.

He'd held the receipt from the Indian restaurant and talked about how deeply he'd connected with her, held a Welcome Center drawstring backpack over his head like all the students had when the sprinklers came on in the ballroom and talked about how he loved her ability to adapt, a LBSU growl towel and talked about watching the sunset with her and their first kiss and how he knew at that moment that he would forever be in love with her.

He'd also talked about their bowling date, her dress, their first dance overlooking the city lights, having dinner with his family, and seeing her at work every day, and how each moment made him fall more hopelessly in love with her. He'd even set the whole video to the music of the playlist they'd danced to on the top of Lookout Hill.

He'd gotten the video all pieced together and had just been adding the music when Deja told him that Summer was on her way. He'd planned to edit it until it was perfect, get the big meeting room decked out with all the objects that had been in the video, and then enlist Valeria's help to get Summer there, but everything was suddenly on a sped-up timeline.

But that was okay. He was adaptable, too.

He'd clicked to generate the movie so he could copy it to his tablet and get it to the big meeting room, hoping it would finish before she arrived. He might have made it, too, but the file had somehow gotten corrupted, and he didn't have the hours it would take to recreate it. Everett had already texted him letting him know that Summer was in the meeting room, and video or not, he wasn't about to waste another minute before telling her how he felt.

He walked from his office to the Welcome Center lobby and then went down the hallway leading to the big meeting room. He stopped just before he got to the door, ran his hands down his shirt and thighs to make sure everything was straight and that his palms weren't sweaty. He probably should've run by the restroom first to check his hair, especially after running his hands through it in corrupted-file-frustration, but he'd just have to hope that it was fine enough—Summer was waiting for him on the other side of the wall.

So he took a deep breath and then walked into the room.

The lights were at half-brightness, but Summer still seemed to glow from where she stood in the middle of the room, right next to a blanket spread on the floor, wearing her Welcome Center polo, dark wash jeans, and blue and yellow-striped wedge heels that were anything but sensible yet so perfectly Summer. She bit her lip, her face showing a tentative hopefulness that he felt in his own expression.

Then a smile quickly spread across her face at seeing him. That smile seemed to write itself on his heart, instantly taking its place in the spot where forever memories resided. She was sheer perfection. He could stand there, soaking her in, always.

But he also needed to talk to her and felt himself being pulled to her. He glanced down at the blanket and the strange pile of vending machine goods on it, making sure he wasn't going to step on it.

Summer glanced down at it, too, and let out a breathy

chuckle. "It's supposed to be a picnic. Those flashlights were going to be candles."

Both their eyes flew to the door as they heard Tess say, "I'm so sorry I'm late. We had Ava's dance recital, and—did we miss it?" She and her husband, Dane, were hurrying into the room, each holding one of their five-year-old's hands.

Pavani shook her head and beckoned them to the back of the room.

Brock looked at the crowd of nine people at the back of the room, all watching them with anticipation and excitement like they were watching the climax of a movie they'd been dying to see. He had asked them all for their help, but he hadn't really anticipated them being in the room for this part. "Is it weird that everyone is here?" It wasn't exactly what he'd envisioned when he'd pictured this moment.

Summer shrugged and nodded. "But it's also nice."

He glanced back at them and nodded, too. It kind of was. It was like he and Summer had their own support section of people they cared about, cheering them on.

"Summer—" he said at the same time Summer said, "I wanted to—"

"You go first," she said.

He nodded. "I made a video for you." Her eyebrows rose in anticipation, so he quickly forged on. "But things didn't quite go according to plan. I wanted to do a big grand gesture—you know, like Lloyd standing outside Diane's window in *Say Anything*, holding up the giant boom box, or when Edward pulled up in a white limo in *Pretty Woman* and ignored his fear of heights to climb up the fire escape to bring flowers to Vivian, or when Max gave Lorelei a thousand yellow daisies in *Gilmore Girls*."

"You watched *Gilmore Girls*?"

"I wanted the perfect way to show you how much I care for you and that I will always be there for you." He knew she would've loved something like that. It would've been right up her alley. Some of the ideas he'd come up with would've been outside of his comfort zone, but that didn't matter if it helped her to know how he felt.

"I wanted to do something that let you know that you are the most incredible woman I've ever known and that I've fallen for you a little more every day. Something to let you know that I won't push; I know it could take a while to truly show you that it's you, Summer. It'll always be you and no one else. Something to show you that I will be here for you in whatever capacity you need me. Something to show you that I love you. I wanted to do something big."

His heart hammered in his ears. He searched her face, wishing he could hear her thoughts and know how she felt about him. About all of this.

She took a quick step forward, closing the gap between them, her hands flying to the sides of his face, her eyes searching his. She pulled one hand back to swipe at a tear that started to run down her cheek, then placed her hand back on the side of his face.

"I don't need something big like that. What's most important is for you to know that I was wrong. So wrong. And so afraid. But I figured everything out. And now I get it, Brock. I get how people can fall in love and know they'll love someone forever. I never really got it before, but I get it now, Brock. I love you, and all that matters is that you know that."

He searched her eyes and saw the conviction behind her words. He put his hands around her waist and pulled her close as her warm, soft lips met his. They had kissed so many times in the past few weeks, but this one felt so different. It felt sure, confident. It felt like promises. It felt like love.

After a long moment that he didn't want to ever end, Summer pulled back and smiled at him. And then everyone in the back of the room—all the people he'd somehow forgotten were even present—started cheering. Loudly. With clapping and shouts and whistling, as if the Aquamoose just scored the winning touchdown.

They both chuckled and glanced down and then just as quickly looked back into each other's eyes, and he wondered if she felt as unwilling as he did to be apart.

She slid her arms around his back and rested her head against his chest, her forehead against his neck, fitting ever so perfectly into the space like they were made for each other. His heart that had been beating so erratically before had calmed, a peaceful right-ness washing over him.

After a moment, he pulled back enough to see Summer's face. "So you wouldn't have wanted some kind of big grand gesture?"

She grinned at him. "Oh, I'm not saying that at all. Will I get to see the video you made later?"

He smiled right back. "I will definitely recreate it for you."

From his peripheral vision, he saw Pavani raise her hand. "Will we get to see it, too?"

He chuckled, shaking his head.

"Okay, okay," Tess said, "let's let them have their picnic in peace. Everybody out. Chop, chop."

Summer held his hand as everyone filed out of the room, smiling at them. Then he turned back to the woman he loved as she pulled him down onto the blanket and scooped the pile of packed snacks closer to them. "This calls for a celebration. Pick your poison."

"I think we need a bigger celebration. How about we order takeout, load our arms full of all of this, go pass it out to as many hungry-looking college students as we can find, then come back here and kiss until the food arrives."

"Ooo. I like the way you think," Summer said, then she leaned across the pile of snacks and gave him a kiss.

Chapter Twenty-Three

SUMMER

Summer stood at the front side of the seated crowd of one hundred fifty prospective students, a couple hundred of their parents and guardians, and all fifty of her ambassadors during the opening session of the second Aquamoose Tracks overnighter of the year, watching Brock on stage. He had tweaked his presentation about scholarships since their first time, five weeks ago now, and the crowd was even more engaged.

For as much as getting up in front of a crowd of people wasn't really his thing, he was remarkably good at it. Probably because he was so passionate about the subject—and it showed.

She also marveled at how much things had changed since Monday when she'd had so many big realizations before laying her heart out for Brock. And then experiencing how sweetly he cared for that heart. She watched him on stage, trying to put a name to the feeling she had experienced with him ever since.

Then it hit her: confidence.

She was now confident in her love for him. Confident in his love for her. There was something remarkable about the feeling that someone would love her unconditionally, no matter what, and she couldn't believe the difference it made. It was something she wasn't sure she had fully experienced with anyone before. She had experienced it to some degree with her dad over the past few years and with friends, especially Valeria. But she'd never felt it this strongly. Not strongly enough to name it.

When Brock finished his presentation and the admitted student who knew her login information stood on the stage, beaming, the crowd enthusiastically applauded right along with her.

Brock walked down the stairs, grinning, and she noticed how the grin changed ever so slightly when his eyes landed on her. The first grin had been for how the crowd had reacted to something that was so important to him. The second grin had been just for her, and she wanted to take a picture and look at it always.

As Pavani took the stage to emcee, Brock walked straight over to Summer and gave her hand a quick squeeze.

"You did good," she whispered, squeezing his hand

back. Then she looked up at the stage. "Remember how, a couple of months ago, we each worried this event wouldn't go well for vastly different reasons?"

He chuckled and reached up to give his glasses a nudge. "And then remember how well it went?" He glanced at the back of the room. "There aren't any kids in here with balloons this time, right?"

She glanced around the room, too, a split second of panic at the memory, even though it wasn't the first time that she had checked since the event started.

"And remember how we disagreed on everything?" he asked.

She shrugged and then winked. "To be honest, we likely still will."

"Well," he said, cocking his head to the side, "maybe not on *everything*. I think we can both agree, for example, that you're about to walk up on stage and capture every-one's heart. And that you're pretty good at that."

She smiled and looked down. "And we can agree that my shoes are pretty spectacular."

He looked at her heeled ankle boots that were a camo pattern, but with an incredibly perfect-for-Aquamoose-Tracks purple and teal color, and nodded. "We can defi-nitely agree on that."

Then she met his eyes. "And that you're a rather smart, generous, kind, gorgeous man."

He gave her a look that made her heart skip a beat—

something he'd been doing frequently enough that she wondered if an entirely new rhythm of her heart was something she needed to ask her doctor about.

She heard Pavani say, "Summer Graham," and realized that she hadn't been listening to anything her friend had been saying on stage, but knew it was time to head up there to give her presentation on all the ways that these students were going to feel right at home at Lake Baldwin State University.

When she got up on stage, she took one last glance at Brock and smiled, knowing that when she finished her presentation, he'd be the one clapping the loudest.

Epilogue

AVERY

"Oh my heck specks, it is cold out there!" Avery said to no one in particular as she stepped into the event center with a crowd of basketball fans dressed in purple and teal. The warm air made her do a full-body shiver as she shook the snow off her coat and stomped her boots on the mats. The snowstorm had only dumped about eight inches today, but the winds were already blowing drifts that were closer to six feet high around the building.

Instead of following the crowds to the ticketing agents at the main doors leading into the arena, she followed the curving hallway around to the other side of the building, where the small gym stood adjacent to the arena. As soon as she walked through the doors, she saw Pavani, Elle, Everett, Deja, Tess, Summer's friend Valeria, and in front of them all, Brock.

She waved to all of them, then walked up to Brock. "Holy donut holes, you're practically glowing! Is it from excitement or nerves?"

He chuckled. "A little of both." He took in a deep breath. "Actually, a *lot* of both."

"Are you ready for this?" She knew Brock didn't love the spotlight like Summer did, and she was so impressed that he would do something this huge for her. Avery didn't know if she would be willing to do the same.

He nodded his head.

"It's going to go great, I know it." She turned to glance at the door, amazed at how much she could hear the crowd even though the game hadn't started yet. "I better get in there and find Summer. Good luck!"

He nodded and said thanks, then Avery headed back around the outer hallway and went through the normal doors into the arena. She immediately spotted the crowd of Aquamoose Tracks students and ambassadors in the section just beside center court. With two hundred of them present, all standing and sitting in the same area, holding their growl towels, and eating Aquamoose Tracks ice cream, it wasn't hard. And once she saw them, she pretty quickly spotted Summer as she made her way up toward the top of the stands, straight up from the students.

When she reached Summer, her friend gave her a hug before they both sat down. "Thank you so much for coming tonight. I didn't think I'd have a problem finding someone in the Welcome Center to take Pavani's place when she said she had to leave to go help a friend. I figured Brock would be here, since he always is, but then his brother had a thing he needed help with, and Elle had some party and Everett said he had to head to his parents', and even Deja had a conflict."

"Wow," Avery said, hoping her voice didn't give anything away. "That's pretty bonkers to have everyone busy on the same night."

"Right?" She pulled out two packages of M&M's and handed one to Avery. "So I'm super grateful that you were willing to come."

After the band finished playing the school's fight song, prompting nearly nine thousand people to join in singing, Summer turned to Avery and asked, "So how's life? Been on any fun adventures lately?" before popping a candy into her mouth.

Avery looked down at her M&M's, tipping the package a bit, watching the colored candies fall over each other. "No adventures. At all." It was probably because it was February—the part of the year when it felt like winter was never going to end and there was nothing fun going on anywhere. "My life has been so boring."

"Well, that needs fixing, ASAP. That's no way to live."

Avery smiled. She liked being around Summer. She made it feel like anything was possible if she was willing to take a step in the right direction. "I've actually been thinking about contacting my friend Nikolas Servais."

Summer grabbed her arm. "The foreign exchange student who lived at your house as a teenager? The one in Belgium?"

Avery grinned. "Yep, that one. He said I could go visit him anytime and he would show me around the place. I don't know, I just feel like I need to do something drastic to get my life out of the rut it's in. Maybe I should do that." She was craving adventure, and that was bigger than any adventure she could imagine. "I'm just nervous."

"About the cost?"

Avery shook her head. "I have enough saved for the plane ticket. And since Nikolas said I could stay in his grandpa's flat, I wouldn't have to pay for lodging. It's just ... I don't know. Big." She didn't do adventures that big. The biggest adventure she'd been on in a long time had been sneaking into her own office area five months ago.

"I want you to think of this," Summer said as they both raised their arms in the air as the wave of raised arms circling the arena circled around their direction. "Imagine that you contacted that sweet boy you knew as a teenager, who is probably just as sweet of a man now, and he—and a girlfriend, you said?—showed you around Belgium and you had the vacation of a lifetime. Now picture yourself a year from now and think about how you would feel."

Avery closed her eyes, imagining exactly that, and let

the emotions that followed sink into her, filling her completely. Without even opening her eyes, she said, "I would feel powerful. Like I could accomplish anything."

"Okay, now imagine you never took that leap to contact Nikolas. Picture yourself a year from now—how would you feel?"

The negative feelings felt so overwhelming that her eyes flew open as if to reassure herself that she wasn't actually experiencing that. "Kind of ... hopeless, I guess." She tried to think about how to explain it. "Like my life was destined to always be boring and unfulfilling. Like not taking that chance would make me not take any future chances, either." Wow. Experiencing both sets of emotions that close together was rather eye-opening.

Based on the smile on Summer's face, she understood exactly what Avery had just experienced. "The bigger the leap, the bigger the payoff. You want an exciting life? Be willing to take the big leap."

Avery grinned. "Okay, I'm going to do it." She hugged her friend because she was suddenly so full of energy and really needed to spend some of it.

The band and the cheering got louder and louder as the last of the people found their seats and the game got closer to starting. Then they introduced the players and it became impossible to talk. She didn't know if it was the fact that she'd made the decision to contact Nikolas or if it was how good the Aquamoose team started playing, but she felt a new energy flowing through her.

This close to the end of the basketball season, everyone seemed to cheer louder, the players played harder, the excitement reaching fevered heights. Especially since the game was so close—the scores were almost never more than two points apart, sometimes for LBSU, sometimes for their opponent.

When the clock counted down closer and closer to the two minutes until halftime mark, Avery kept glancing at the group of ambassadors and prospective students, the anticipation nearly killing her. By the way several of the ambassadors kept glancing at the game clock, she knew that they were feeling it, too.

When the clock hit the two-minute mark, all fifty ambassadors stood up, and the one hundred fifty prospective students stood soon after. Then they started filing toward the nearest aisle.

Summer immediately stood, too. "Where are they going?" She glanced over at Avery like she needed someone else to verify the baffling scene before her, so Avery stood. "Is this some kind of mutinous exodus?" She started scooting toward the side to make her way to the steps going down. But Avery stood on that side of Summer, so she surreptitiously slowed her progress. "They can't just leave; I'm responsible for those kids. So are the ambassadors.

They need to be where their parents are expecting them to be."

Jessa, one of the ambassadors, turned around just then and, in exaggerated motions, mouthed to Summer over the roaring crowd, *It's all good.* With both hands, she motioned for her to sit down. *You stay there.*

It was fortunate that it was Jessa who they picked to tell Summer to stay where she was because she might've been the only one who could've stopped Summer. She didn't exactly sit down, though. She stayed standing, watching as they exited the arena in one long line.

"Come on," Avery said. "Let's sit. I'm sure everything's okay or Jessa wouldn't be going along with it."

That seemed to calm Summer enough to get her to sit. But the moment the halftime buzzer sounded, Summer stood again and started shuffling to the side, trying to get Avery to shuffle toward the stairs again. "There's no way they all wanted to get concessions or that they all needed to go to the restrooms. I should go check on them."

"Summer, I'm sure everything is fine." There were other people on their row who were standing and not moving toward the stairs quickly, which definitely helped. Avery was doing the minimum shuffling she could do without outright stopping Summer, but it wasn't enough. The people in the row in front of them had mostly vacated for halftime, so Summer stepped over their seats and onto their row so she could get to the stairs more quickly.

Avery stepped over onto the row below, as well. She hadn't wanted to join the others down on the court for the halftime show, where all eyes would be on them, and thought she'd gotten the much easier job in helping with Brock's plan. But she hadn't anticipated how strong Summer's will to leave would be.

Once Summer got to the section where all the prospective students and ambassadors had been sitting that was now vacant, Avery did the only thing she could think of to stall her friend until everyone could make it to the court. She pretended to twist her ankle, yelped in pain, and collapsed into a crouch, both hands encircling her ankle, holding on tight. Summer immediately dropped to a crouch beside her. "Are you okay?"

She managed to wince and attempt to move it for long enough to keep Summer's attention until she saw from the corner of her eye that everyone was making their way onto the court for the halftime show. Then she dropped the act and pointed. "There they are!"

They both stood and watched as the cheer team flipped and bounced and jogged and high-kicked their way onto the center of the court, while all two hundred of the students under Summer's care walked out onto the court, splitting into two lines as they made their way across the back, front, and sides of the court, each holding two two-foot square cards in their hands. Once they were in place, they all set their cards on the ground and stood at attention.

"They're helping the cheerleaders with the halftime show?" Summer asked. "That is so great! But why did no one come to me to get it cleared? It makes no sense. Do you think they cleared it with Pavani and she just forgot to tell me?"

Avery just shrugged, not even caring that she couldn't hide her smile. This was something worth smiling about. "I guess."

"Why didn't Jessa tell me?"

Then booming music started, and the cheer team started doing their choreographed dance and acrobatics routine. They did kicks and basket tosses and stood on each other's shoulders and bodies were flipping and being tossed into the air and caught again to perfect rhythm and fully synchronized as the music blared and the students waited, their hands clasped behind their backs.

As soon as the music stopped, the cheerleaders started doing some LBSU cheers, getting the crowd involved and shouting cheers right along with them. Then, all the students along the perimeter picked up their signs at a signal from one of the cheerleaders.

"When did they have time to practice this?" Summer asked. "I've been with them every moment since they stepped on campus earlier today."

Then the cheerleaders started doing a cheer that they'd never done before. As one, all the cheerleaders called out "S, U, M, M, E, R, Graham," and with each letter and word, the Aquamoose Tracks students along the backside held up their signs, each with one letter spelling out Summer's name.

Well, mostly—one of the students holding an M had it upside down and had to turn it around, and the student that should've been holding the H was holding a Y. But at the nudging of the person standing next to him, he quickly switched the card with the one on the ground, and it spelled her name. They were actually doing pretty well since none of the prospective students even knew about this until the ambassadors spread the word after they'd been seated at the game.

Avery watched Summer's face as she took it in, confusion and bafflement covering her features. The cheerleaders continued calling out the next part of their cheer, "Come on down." The students at the front of the court held up signs spelling out *Come on down.* All the cheerleaders were looking right at Summer and waving their poms, gesturing for her to come down.

Six cheerleaders went to the front of the court, just below the center aisle, forming two lines of three, making an aisle for Summer to walk through once she'd made it down from the stands and onto the court. But she still seemed too stunned to move, just staring at her name in big letters on the court.

So Avery hooked her arm in Summer's and started leading her to the center aisle. Then she led her down the steps toward the court. She kept sneaking glances at Summer's face, which clearly showed that she didn't have a clue what was going on.

Summer turned to Avery. "Do you know what's happening?"

Avery shrugged. "I think we should go find out."

As they got past most of the crowd and stepped onto the court, she knew the moment Summer spotted Deja, Elle, Everett, Pavani, Tess, and Valeria standing in the line with the ambassadors. Summer just pointed at them, mouth open, no words coming out. Avery took her spot with the others as the cheerleaders whisked Summer out to the center of the court.

Avery glanced up at the JumboTron, which was capturing Summer's confusion for all to see. Deja grabbed her arm. "Isn't this the most exciting thing ever?"

Avery grinned and nodded.

One of the cheerleaders had a microphone and she said, "Okay, I need everyone to give me the best drumroll you've got! So hit your hands on your thighs, stomp your feet, just make sure you're giving us some noise!"

The arena erupted in loud, pounding, rhythmic sounds. And then the cheerleaders in a line between Summer and the line of ambassadors and students parted and Brock walked forward. Summer's hands flew to her mouth, her knees weakening, causing her to bend over, slightly crouched. From the JumboTron, Avery could see that tears were streaming down her face.

Brock stopped about five feet in front of Summer, and the cheerleader with the microphone handed it to him. He looked up at the crowds of people in the stands. "Hello, Lake Baldwin State University students! All you freshmen, sophomores, and juniors out there—if you came on a campus tour or did the Aquamoose Tracks overnighter before becoming a student here, then you have met Summer Graham. In fact, you probably remember her playing a part in helping you make the huge, life-changing decision to come to Lake Baldwin State University."

The crowd was so hyped up from the game and was so invested in what was happening that they were all cheering loudly. He waited for them to quiet a bit, then his eyes landed on Summer and he said, "She's helped me make some huge, life-changing decisions, too."

Then he got down on one knee, and the crowd erupted in cheers. Avery placed her hands steepled over her nose and mouth, pressing on her sinuses in an attempt to stop her own tears from falling, but they fell anyway.

"Summer," Brock said, "if there's one thing I've learned this school year, it's that I want to be with you forever. Will you marry me?"

At that cue, all the ambassadors and students spread

out in a line behind Brock held up their second big card, spelling out the words *Will you marry me?*

Summer batted at the tears on her cheeks with one hand, then said, "Yes! Of course I will!" Then she fell to her knees in front of him, grabbed his face, and started kissing him.

The cameraman zoomed in on the two of them, and nine thousand people gave a collective "*Aww!*"

Then Brock pulled a ring box out of his pocket and slipped the ring in it onto Summer's finger. The speakers started blasting a song about falling in love and the crowd was all clapping, but all Avery could do was watch the joy that was emanating off Brock and Summer on the Jumbo-Tron. They looked so happy she could hardly stand it.

The cheerleaders waved their poms and Avery and everyone who worked in the Welcome Center directed the prospective students and ambassadors up the center aisle and back to the section where they'd been seated.

Once they were seated, Avery, along with everyone who worked in the Welcome Center and Brock and Summer, headed up to the row of seats reserved for them. Summer and Brock took their seats in the middle of all of them, looking at each other with such happy eyes.

Back when Summer and Brock had first started being interested in each other, Avery had noticed a change in their smiles. In looking at them now, she could see that their smiles now reached a whole new level. She felt like her whole body was smiling just seeing how happy they were.

As she watched them, she began to feel an ache deep inside her. She really wanted that for herself at some point. But she also knew, deep in her core, that if her life stayed on the same path it was on, she would never get it. She needed to make a big change. She needed to get on the path that would help her get there.

And she could also feel, deep in her core, that the first step was to contact her friend Nikolas and to set the trip into motion that was, hopefully, going to change everything.

She looked back over at Summer, thinking about Brock's words about how many people Summer had helped to make life-changing decisions in their lives, and realized that her friend was helping her to make her own life-changing decision.

And she realized that she was ready to take that big leap.

WANT to find out what happens? Tap to read all about Avery and Nikolas in *It Started with a Note*.

Author's note:

I have never worked in a Welcome Center or in the Admissions Department of a university, so I sought help from people who have.

I visited a bunch of colleges (experiencing firsthand SO many campus tours! But not nearly as many as Summer ;)) and found a university that had the feel that I wanted my fictional Lake Baldwin State University to have.

That college was Southern Utah University, and I owe them a huge debt of gratitude. Their Welcome Center and Admissions Department let me travel to their school and they so graciously and helpfully spent two days talking with me about what they do. They were so instrumental in helping me more authentically portray the jobs of the people who worked there.

None of the characters in this book are based on the people who work there, and any mistakes are definitely my own. But they deserve a massive huge thank you! This book wouldn't be what it is without them.

—Meg

It Started with a Note

More small-town romance from Meg Easton

Second Chance on the Corner of Main Street
Christmas at the End of Main Street
More than Friends in the Middle of Main Street
Love Again at the Heart of Main Street
More than Enemies on the Bridge of Main Street
Coming Home to the Top of Main Street

More titles from Meg

How to Not Fall for the Guy Next Door
How to Not Fall for the Wrong Guy
How to Not Fall for Your Best Friend
How to Not Fall for Your Ex

Get COMING HOME TO THE TOP
OF MAIN STREET free when you join
Meg's VIP readers!

JOIN MEG'S NEWSLETTER AT WWW.MEGEASTON.COM

Meg Easton writes contemporary sweet and clean romance. She lives at the foot of a mountain with her name on it (or at least one letter of her name) in Utah. She loves gardening, bike riding, baking, swimming before the sun rises, and spending time with her husband and three kids.

She can be found online at www.megeaston.com, where

you can sign up to receive her newsletter and stay up to date with new releases, get exclusive bonus content, and more.

If you liked this book please leave a review. Your review can help other readers find books they might fall in love with.

facebook.com/MegEastonBooks